Winner Books are produced by Victor Books and are designed to entertain and instruct young readers in Christian principles.

Other Winner Books you will enjoy:

W9-BZZ-463

GRACE FOX ANDERSON is publication editor of *Counselor,* Scripture Press' take-home paper for children 9 to 11. She has been in church-related work with children for more than 25 years. Mrs. Anderson received her degree in Christian education from Wheaton College, Wheaton, Ill. She has edited and compiled the stories in the popular Winner Books' Animal Tails Series: *The Hairy Brown Angel and Other Animal Tails, The Peanut Butter Hamster, Skunk for Rent, The Incompetent Cat, The Duck Who Had Goosebumps, The Pint-Sized Piglet,* and *The Hopeless Hen.*

THE
PEANUT
BUTTER
HAMSTER
and Other Animal Tails

edited by Grace Fox Anderson
illustrated by Richard Johnson

A WINNER BOOK

VICTOR BOOKS®
A DIVISION OF SCRIPTURE PRESS PUBLICATIONS INC.
USA CANADA ENGLAND

CREDITS: "Mr. Owl," "My Little Hamster," "Playful Water Clown"—previously published in *Story Friends*, published by The Mennonite Publishing House. "The Gift," "The Ostrich," "My Pet Turtle"—previously published in *The Young Soldier*, published by The Salvation Army. "Killer Coon," "The Lost Kitten," "Speedy," "Starlight," "Five Creatures God Used," " 'I'll Never Forgive Him!' " "A Sheep Called Sheba," "A Sack Full of Kittens," "A Whale Out of Water," "In Three Mighty Leaps," "Trouble for Biddy," "Fourteen Days in an Attic"—all previously published in *Counselor*, published by Scripture Press Publications, Inc.

Scripture is from the *King James Version* unless otherwise indicated. The other version quoted with permission is the *New American Standard Bible* (NASB), © the Lockman Foundation 1960, 1962, 1963, 1968, 1971, 1972, 1973, 1975, 1977.

Library of Congress Catalog Card No. 78-65204
ISBN: 0-88207-484-9

Twelfth printing, 1988

VICTOR BOOKS
A division of SP Publications, Inc.
Wheaton, Ill. 60187

CONTENTS

The Peanut Butter Hamster

A TRUE STORY by Gloria Truitt

"MOTHER, WHERE'S MY COAT?" yelled Laura as she bounded into the kitchen.

"In the family room closet! Now hurry, or we'll be late for church," called Mother.

The Truitt family stood in the kitchen waiting for Laura to find her coat. Suddenly they heard a frantic cry from the family room. "Oh, no! Dusty's gone!"

At once, Mother, Daddy, and Laura's brother Johnny ran to the family room. Laura was staring tearfully at her hamster's empty cage.

It was obvious how Dusty, the hamster, had gotten out. Someone had left the screen cover off the large, glass hamster house. It wasn't important to find out who had been careless. But it was important to find Dusty.

Daddy quickly organized the search. "I'll check the

7

closet," he said. "The rest of you look under the furniture."

They all knew that a hamster could squeeze through a hole as small as a nickel. Where could she have gone?

Daddy shook out every boot and shoe. He moved the camera case, movie screen, and sewing machine box out of the closet. Only after he had inspected every inch did he say, "Well, Dusty isn't in here. I guess we'd better search the whole house."

Upstairs and down, the family hunted beneath every piece of furniture and behind every door. They looked in each closet, cabinet, and box, but Dusty was nowhere to be found.

Finally, Mother said, "Don't worry. We'll find her after church, but we'd better leave now, or we'll be very late."

All through Sunday School, Laura thought about her little lost hamster. During prayer time, the other children joined Laura in asking God to help her find Dusty.

After church, Laura and Johnny found their parents in the church hallway talking to Dr. and Mrs. Ryan. "Hello," said Laura. "Aren't you an animal doctor?"

"Yes, I am," Dr. Ryan answered. "Do you have a sick animal, Laura?"

"No," Laura replied. "I have a *lost* one!"

"Oh, that's too bad," Dr. Ryan said. "What kind of an animal is it, and where did you lose it?"

"She's Dusty, my pet hamster," Laura said. "This

morning when we were getting ready for church, we found that she had gotten out of her cage. We've looked everywhere but can't find her. Do you think she's gone forever?"

Dr. Ryan put his arm around Laura and said, "I'll tell you what to do. As soon as you get home, take a little saucer and put a big glob of peanut butter on it. Then place it in the middle of your floor. If Dusty is still running around the house, she'll smell the peanut butter and come to it. Hamsters can't resist peanut butter, you know."

"Oh, thank-you very much!" Laura cried. Then turning to Mother and Daddy, she said, "Hurry! Let's go home right now! I can't wait to dish out that peanut butter for Dusty!"

When they got home, Laura put a glob of peanut butter on a dish and set it in the middle of the living room floor. After lunch, she settled down on the sofa to wait and watch. But no hamster showed up. The afternoon crept by slowly. Still, no Dusty!

Once in a while a tear rolled down Laura's cheek, and she quickly brushed it away with the back of her hand. "Why doesn't God answer my prayers and bring Dusty back?" she asked Daddy.

"Well, honey, we must trust God to do what is best. We know that He loves us, and He loves little animals too. Why don't you stop worrying, and start believing that God will return Dusty to us?"

"Do you really think He will?" Laura asked.

"Of course!" Father answered with a smile. "I've never had the slightest doubt!"

Laura jumped up from the sofa and hugged Daddy. "Yippee!" she squealed happily. "I feel so much better now! Will you watch the peanut butter for a little while? I think I'll go and play with my dolls."

It was an hour later—nearly dinnertime when Mother called Laura to wash her hands and help set the table. Daddy had been reading a book, but had not forgotten to glance now and then at the glob of peanut butter.

Laura entered the living room and said, "Dinner's ready, Daddy. I'll put your book away for you." As she replaced the book on the bottom shelf, she thought she saw something move.

Yes, indeed she did! Coming out of a little hole at the bottom of the bookcase, and heading straight for the peanut butter, was Dusty! Laura carefully scooped up her pet with both hands and gently hugged her. "Look," she cried. "God *did* return Dusty to us!"

After dinner the family discussed how God had answered Laura's prayers. "I'm sure God planned our talk with Dr. Ryan," Mother said. "Without the peanut butter, Dusty might not have found her way out of the bookcase."

"God did help us in the best way, didn't He!" Laura said. Then she looked through the kitchen door at Dusty, now busily washing herself in her cage. Laura laughed happily as she said, "Look how dirty she got under that bookcase! Dusty *really* is Dusty now, isn't she?"

My Little Hamster

by Gloria Truitt

I have a furry hamster with
   The strangest silly ways.
Throughout the day she likes to sleep,
   And in the night she plays!
She runs for miles upon a wheel,
   But doesn't seem to care
That she remains in the same old place,
   Not going anywhere!
Now, when it's time for her to eat,
   She has two pouches that
She fills up like big pillows till
   Her cheeks are stuffed and fat!
Though she has silly ways, she is
   As gentle as can be.
I love my little hamster, and
   I know that she loves me!

Killer Coon

A FICTION STORY by Ralph L. Bartholomew

WHEN they got back from town, Jim Thompson and his dad unloaded their pickup truck. They piled the heavy feed bags in the barn, then carried the groceries into the kitchen. When the groceries were put away and other Saturday night chores done, Jim was ready for bed.

"Well, Son, think we'll catch that old coon tonight?" his dad said.

Jim grinned and forgot about being tired. Then he remembered. "But, Dad, I should get some sleep tonight so I can get up for Sunday School tomorrow."

His father looked at him wearily. "Five days a week you go to school and can't help me on the farm. Five nights I can't take you coon hunting 'cause you'll fall asleep in class the next day. Now you've got this idea you have to go to church all the time!

"Look, Jim, I'm not saying you've got to go hunting. It just isn't easy for me to track around the woods alone all night with my bad knee. That coon's killed a lot of our chickens and the best hunting dog I ever owned. I'm going to get him."

Jim knew what he must do. "OK, Dad, I'll be ready in a minute."

"Good boy," his father said, grinning. "I'll go get my rifle."

In his room, Jim got his rifle, a box of shells, and a big flashlight. It wasn't that he didn't want to go on the hunt with his dad. But since he'd received Christ as his Saviour at a campout last winter, he'd enjoyed the Bible study in Sunday School and church. His father couldn't understand. He'd never been to church and didn't feel Jim needed to go either.

"Please, Lord," Jim whispered before he left his room, "help us catch that old coon quickly so I can get some sleep and get up for church in the morning."

A few minutes later, Jim, his dad, and their new young hunting hound, Bess, were walking through the woods. It was spring. The air was cool and sweet and the moon was bright. They planned to look for the trail down by the creek.

As they walked, Jim remembered the last time they'd hunted the old coon. The wily animal had plunged into a deep pool in the creek and headed for the other side. Their dog Queenie splashed in after it. The coon turned around in midstream and waited. When the dog swam up, the coon climbed on her head and held it under water.

By the time Jim and his dad got there, it was too late. The dog had drowned. Now as they neared the creek again, Jim watched the new hound and wondered.

"See how she sniffs the ground?" his dad said proudly. "Yes, sir, I think young Bess here will turn out to be an even better hunter than old Queenie. That is, once I get her trained."

So Dad was beginning to love this new hound as he had once loved old Queenie, Jim thought.

When they reached the creek, Jim could see the moonlight sparkling on the water. They flashed their lights on the ground until they found the coon tracks. "Look, Dad," Jim said. "It's the killer coon's trail all right. See the print—only three toes on the right front foot."

Bess caught the scent and was off. Jim ran after her, his Dad following as fast as he could with a bad leg.

The trail led down the path for a short way, then circled around through the woods. Suddenly the dog let out a long howl, "Arrr . . . rrr . . . rrr!"

"Come on, Dad," Jim yelled. "I think we've got it treed!"

Jim crashed ahead through the bushes until he caught up with the young hound. Bess was at the bottom of a big oak tree, howling wildly. In another minute, his dad was by his side.

"Think the coon's up there, Dad?" Jim panted.

"Don't know," his Dad said. "Flash your light around in the branches. Let's see if we can find it."

They both ran their lights up and down the lower limbs of the tree. Then they turned off the lights and studied the tree in the moonlight, thinking they might see the big fellow's silhouette.

"Nothing that looks like a coon up there," his dad said finally. "Could be hiding way up high, I suppose."

"Maybe it ran out to the end of a branch and jumped," Jim suggested.

"Wouldn't be the first time a coon did that," his dad said. "That's one of their favorite tricks. Why don't you get Bess away from the trunk. Take her far out under the branches."

Jim took the dog and started her sniffing in a large circle around the tree. Once she caught the scent, but it led her right back to the tree. Jim had to start her again. Suddenly Bess found the trail.

In a few minutes, the trio was crashing through the dark woods again, headed back toward the creek. Bess was in the lead. Jim was close behind, and his dad was following as fast as he could.

The crisp, cool air of the night made Jim's blood tingle. Suddenly Bess gave another yelp, then started baying eagerly.

Again, the coon had chosen a large oak tree to hide in. Jim and his dad flashed their lights around the branches for a while. But they could see no sign of the wary animal.

"Think he's tricked us again?" Jim asked.

"Don't know," his dad answered. "Let's look a bit more before we give up."

Just then they heard a crash in the brush. The old

coon must have hidden far out on the end of a limb and jumped. Young Bess yelped happily and dashed off toward the noise.

Jim followed, almost falling flat as he tripped over a vine. Suddenly he went cold. The coon was heading for the creek with the young dog right after it. The coon had tricked the wise old hunting dog. Young Bess wouldn't have a chance.

"Bess! Bess!" Jim yelled as he half ran, half slid down the steep slope to the creek. "No, Bess! Come back!"

But the dog was already in the water, splashing and paddling. She could never hear him now.

Jim could see the water shining in the moonlight. The coon was heading for the middle. Paddling close behind was young Bess—too close for Jim to risk a shot at the coon. Maybe Dad could get him. He was an expert shot. But where was Dad? He'd be heartbroken if he lost another dog.

Jim dropped his rifle, pulled off his shoes and jacket, and plunged in. The water was icy. He gasped for breath but could think of only one thing: He could see only one head above water—the coon's. It was drowning Bess!

Just as he reached the middle, he heard his dad sliding down the slope behind him. Underwater, he grabbed the dog's tail and pulled. Bess was fighting to come up for air, but the big coon held on. He couldn't free the dog that way.

Treading water, Jim reached over and grabbed the coon by the tail. With a mighty tug, he pulled the fighting animal off the dog's head, holding it up in the air. Up came Bess, sputtering and gasping for air. Vaguely, Jim heard his dad call and knew the dog had headed for shore.

But he was in trouble now. The coon was clawing and biting at him. Jim still had it by the tail and stretched his arm as far out as he could, but he was cold and tired and his hand was weakening. The coon was trying to inch closer, churning up the water in front of Jim's face.

Suddenly, Jim heard a shot. The coon jerked out

of his hand and fell heavily into the water. Jim turned immediately toward shore.

"You all right, Jim?" his father called, wading out to get him. But even before Jim could answer, his dad's strong arms were lifting him out of the water.

"Jim . . . ," he was saying. "Don't ever do a fool thing like that again! I can get another dog, but not another son." He got Jim ashore and wrapped him in his own warm, dry jacket. "Just don't ever do anything like that again," he muttered gruffly.

They trudged along in silence most of the way with a very wet and subdued Bess following at their heels.

When they reached the cornfield, his dad put his arm around Jim.

"I didn't mean to scold you so," he said quietly. "You did a brave thing, saving our dog's life. But, Jim, don't ever risk your life like that again. Not just for a dog. Remember, you're all I've got now with your mother gone. I love you more than anything else in life."

He was quiet for a long time. They were near the house when he spoke again: "You were telling me the other day how God gave His only Son so men could go to heaven."

"Yeah, Dad, that's right!" Jim answered wonderingly.

"You know, Jim, I'd never really thought before what that meant to God. I think I'd like to get to know more about a God like that."

A sweet, warm happiness filled Jim as they stepped into their old farmhouse.

Speedy

A TRUE STORY by Delores E. Bius

ROGER BIUS sat beside his terrarium and looked in-
tently at Speedy, his pet chameleon. Speedy simply
wasn't living up to his name. Usually he would leap
up and snatch the mealworms Roger fed him. Or he'd
crawl happily around his home, defying gravity by
clinging upside down to the top of the terrarium.

Now Speedy lay, almost unmoving, for hours on
end.

Roger went out to the kitchen to find his mother.
"Mom," he said, "I think there's something really
wrong with Speedy. He must be sick."

His mother turned from the sink and dried her
hands. "Are you sure?" she asked with a concerned
frown. "Let's go look at him."

After examining the tiny fellow, his mother agreed.
"I'm afraid you're right, Son. Ordinarily when we take

the top off, he tries to jump out. But he's hardly paying attention to us. What does your book about chameleons say?"

"It says we could give him sugar water but I already tried that. And I also put my desk lamp on close to the terrarium to keep him warm. The book says to do that if he has a cold."

"Well, Roger, maybe he caught cold when the weather changed," his mother said. "I'm sure he'll be himself in a day or so."

Mother was usually right. But days passed and Speedy became weaker. He wouldn't eat and seemed to be losing weight. One day, Roger noticed a lump appearing over one of Speedy's eyes.

On Saturday he and his mother went to the pet shop. The man in charge told them to try Tetracycline (teh-tra-SIGH-klen) and sold them a capsule for a dime. He carefully explained how to open the capsule and mix a little of the powder with water and spray it on Speedy. He said he usually gave it to other animals, so it might help lizards too. He also suggested putting Mercurochrome (mer-CURE-ah-krome) on the lump over Speedy's eye.

Roger came home from the pet shop, happy. He was sure the medicine would bring Speedy back to his playful self again.

However, several days later, Speedy could hardly lift his head to lap the sugar water Roger gave him. Roger held his pet in his hand and stroked him carefully. The poor little fellow was so thin, his tiny bones stuck out of his tight skin. His head with the large lump over one eye looked huge and grotesque.

One night at supper, Roger asked his father, "Daddy, I'm so worried about Speedy. He's getting worse. Do you think we could take him to an animal doctor?"

"Roger, I'm sorry but we hardly have money for our own doctor bills. We just don't have it for an animal. If he were a dog, it might not be so bad, but to pay a large fee for Speedy—well I'm afraid not, Son."

"Could I talk to a doctor on the telephone? He

wouldn't charge for that, would he?" Roger asked.

"Well, maybe not," his father agreed.

With his mother's help, Roger found the phone number of a veterinarian and dialed it carefully. The doctor was very kind. He suggested that Roger put a hot compress on Speedy's lump. Roger made a tiny compress out of a cotton ball and applied it regularly. But he still saw no improvement in Speedy.

Then Roger's teacher suggested that he phone the zoo and ask someone in the reptile house for advice. Roger did so. The man at the zoo said Speedy might have pneumonia. "Keep the terrarium extra warm," he suggested, "and you might try feeding him flies since he is probably too weak to eat mealworms."

Again, Roger's spirits rose and he busily caught a number of flies. But Speedy wouldn't eat them either.

Several days later, he picked up his weakened pet and in spite of his 11 years, started to cry. Just then his mother walked into his room. "Why, Roger," she said, "you mustn't cry so. I'm sure Speedy isn't in any pain and you're doing all you can for him."

"But, Mom, it isn't enough. He's not getting well," Roger groaned.

"Son, have you prayed for Speedy?" his mother asked. She knew Roger loved Jesus, and their family prayed about any problem.

"Why, sure, Mom. I prayed for him when he first got sick. Why doesn't God answer my prayers? Is it because animals don't have souls or go to heaven?"

"Roger, we don't know why God doesn't always heal sick people or sick animals. We do know He expects us to see doctors and take medicine and pray. We also know from the Scriptures that even though animals do not have souls, God cares for them. We read in the Bible that not one sparrow falls from the sky without God knowing about it.

"But God doesn't always heal people. I know we hate to see them die, but when they are very sick, death ends their suffering and pain on earth. If they are trusting Jesus as Saviour, they have only joy ahead in heaven.

"Perhaps we should pray that if Speedy isn't going to get well, God will let him die quickly. The poor little fellow is so thin and weak. I know it hurts you to see him so sick."

While Roger tenderly held Speedy, he and his mother prayed together, putting Speedy in God's hands. Somehow, Roger's heart felt lighter when he went to sleep that night. He knew that God was kind and always did what was best for people and animals.

In the morning, Roger looked in the terrarium to check on Speedy. He noticed that his pet was quieter than usual. When he picked up Speedy, he realized that his chameleon had died in the night. God had released the little lizard from its illness and relieved Roger's agony at watching his pet suffer.

Roger was sorry to have Speedy die, but he was glad that the little fellow's pain was over. He went to tell his mother and asked her for a small box to put Speedy in. After he had buried his pet in the backyard, he and his mother prayed. They thanked God for caring about boys and pets, and they both felt better.

The Lost Kitten

A FICTION STORY by Doris L. Kersting

THE gray and white kitten arched its back against Sheri's leg and purred loudly. "See how happy it is!" Sheri cried. Her face glowed. "And see what blue eyes it has, Mama. Not green, like most cats."

"It certainly belongs to someone, dear," Mother said. "Where did you find it?"

"Down in the field all by itself," Sheri answered. "I want to keep it, Mama, please."

"Yes, Mama," added Tommy, Sheri's younger brother, "please let us keep it."

"You'll have to try to find the owner first," Mother said. "Some boy or girl is probably crying because the kitten is lost."

"It could belong to Eileen," Sheri said, remembering. "She told me her mother was going to get her a gray and white kitten."

"Then perhaps you'd better take it to her house and see if it's hers," Mother said. She went back into the house then, as if the matter were ended.

Sheri picked up the kitten, and it snuggled happily under her chin. "Oh, you dear, sweet kitty," she said. "I'm going to keep you, no matter what."

For several minutes she stood and cuddled the kitten. "Can I go with you?" Tommy begged as she finally started across the yard.

"No, Tommy. You stay here," she said.

Sheri walked down the street toward Eileen's house. When she was sure no one at home would see her, she turned the corner. On the next street was a small park. There she sat down in the grass under a large tree and played with the kitten. She laughed with delight as the kitten jumped around. It was trying to catch the dancing shadows the leaves made on the ground when the wind blew.

When it seemed as if enough time had passed for Sheri to have gone to Eileen's and back, she got up. She walked up the alley behind her own house to the garage.

Fortunately, Daddy had been building some shelves in the garage and was parking in the alley each night. She pushed the kitten into the garage and closed the door. The kitten mewed when she started away.

"Shhh, kitty," Sheri whispered to the kitten behind the closed door. "Don't make any noise. I'll bring you some milk when it gets dark."

Sheri went back down the alley and around the corner, then down the street to her house. As she came into the yard, Tommy ran to meet her. "Was it Eileen's kitten?" he asked.

Sheri nodded, but looked at the ground.

"I knew it," Tommy said sadly. "But come and see what we've got for supper—something you like."

"Lasagna?" Sheri guessed, but she didn't hurry.

Tommy nodded. "Mother made it 'cause she knew how disappointed you were about the kitten."

"Oh," Sheri said in a small voice.

Mother looked up as Sheri came into the kitchen. "Was it Eileen's cat?" she asked.

Again Sheri nodded. She didn't look at Mother, but began setting the table.

The lasagna didn't taste as good as usual to Sheri, although Tommy and Daddy said it was the best they'd ever eaten. After supper Sheri helped Mother do the dishes without being asked. Then she read Tommy a story.

When it was dark, she slipped out to the garage with a cup of milk and a saucer. She opened the garage door and called, "Here, Kitty. Here's some nice milk." She poured the milk into the saucer and the kitten came running out of a dark corner. It purred hard as it lapped up the milk.

"Be careful," Sheri whispered, giggling. "You'll burst your purring machine."

When the kitten was through with the milk, it washed its face and paws. Sheri picked it up and it licked her face with its rough little tongue.

Sheri almost forgot that her parents would wonder where she was so long. She put the kitten back in the garage and hurried back to the house. She would come back later and get the kitten when everyone was asleep.

When Sheri burst into the house, her cheeks were rosy from the cool air. She could feel her mother looking at her. "Mother, I found the Big Dipper and Little Dipper!" she exclaimed.

"Stargazing?" her father asked, laughingly and pinched her ear.

Sheri went to her room as soon as she could. She turned out the light and waited by the window until Mother and Daddy went to bed. She wondered if Eileen was lying awake, crying because her kitten was gone.

At last, when she was sure her parents were asleep, she tiptoed out of the house. She hurried to the garage and opened the door. She was afraid to go in, it was so dark. "Here, Kitty, Kitty," she called.

Finally, the kitten came tumbling up to her. Sheri scooped it up and hurried back to the house and her room. She put the kitten on her bed and knelt down to pray. However, she couldn't think of a thing to say so she got into bed with a big sigh.

She tried to play with the purring kitten but it soon fell asleep. Sheri lay awake for a long time. She thought about all the lies she had told.

The next morning the kitten woke her up. Sheri felt happy at the thought of a beautiful new day. She jumped out of bed and went to the window. Just then she saw Eileen Parker's brother out delivering papers. Remembering Eileen gave her a sick feeling in her stomach. She turned away from the window.

Suddenly she had an idea. She grabbed up the kitten, slipped out of her room and out the front door, and put the kitten down in the yard. She'd let Mother think it had come back again today, and this time she would really take it home and leave it there.

Sheri went back to her room and got dressed. Then she set the table for breakfast. Her parents weren't up yet but Tommy was. Suddenly she heard his excited voice just outside the screen door. "It came back, Sheri!" he called. "It came back!" And in he trotted with the kitten in his arms.

Just then mother came into the kitchen. "Well, well," she said, "I guess that kitten must enjoy our company."

Before breakfast, Daddy read a chapter from the Bible. Each of the family prayed until it was Sheri's turn. "Go ahead," Daddy said to her.

"I can't," Sheri said in a choked voice.

"You can't? Why not?" he asked in surprise.

"If you're feeling so bad about the kitten, Sheri," her mother said, "I'm sure we don't mind you having one of your own."

"No, no," Sheri said. "It isn't that. It's—it's—" She raised her head and looked at her parents. "I didn't take it back. I just pretended to."

"Well," Mother said quietly, "there's today yet."

Relief flooded Sheri. "Yes," she said, "I'll take it back right after breakfast." Then she bowed her head again and asked Jesus to forgive her for keeping something that didn't belong to her and for lying about it. It wasn't hard to pray now.

Eileen must have seen Sheri because she came running down the street to meet her. "Is this your kitten?" Sheri called, holding up the furry animal.

Eileen ran up. "You found it!" she exclaimed. "Isn't that something! I got it for you, Sheri. Mama's friend had two to give away. Come and see mine. I didn't know what had happened to yours. I was just out searching for it. Imagine it coming down the street to your house—as if it knew where it belonged!"

Sheri couldn't say a word for a minute. "Oh, Eileen, thank you!" she cried when she recovered from her surprise. "He's just darling. I love him. Now show me yours."

Once more the day seemed beautiful and bright. Sheri's own kitten snuggled in her arms and stuck his little pink nose into the crook of her arm as she followed Eileen into the Parker house.

Mister Owl

by Gloria A. Truitt

An owl is thought to be quite wise
Because he has enormous eyes.
But other birds are just as smart . . .
Not setting Mister Owl apart.
Some owls will measure two feet tall,
And some, six inches. Now that's small!
All the owls are birds of prey,
But rarely do they hunt during day.
Because they have fantastic sight,
They catch and eat their food at night.
One evening I heard hooting sounds,
And ran right home in leaps and bounds.
Mom laughed, " 'Twas just an owl you heard—
Not a monster—just a bird!"

Tusker and Flicka Fight the Cobras

A TRUE STORY by Delores Elaine Bius

NOT all missionaries need to worry about snakes. But Jean and Bob Williams do. They live and serve the Lord in Kenya, East Africa on the north shore of the Indian Ocean, and must continually watch for snakes.

For instance, one morning as Jean reached for a cooking pan on a shelf, she found a small black snake wrapped around the handle. Her husband, Bob, killed it with a knife.

Another time, she was sweeping the floor and discovered a small red snake staring at her from under the baseboard inside the house. She picked up a can of Raid and sprayed it at the snake's head. It crawled under the wood and hasn't come out since, so they hope it is dead.

Since the Williamses are near the African Gariama village, they have two German shepherd dogs to help

keep away thieves at night. The dogs have also kept away snakes! And the Williamses thank God for these furry "guardian angels."

One night when they were ready to go to bed, they heard their large male dog, Tusker, barking and barking. Usually it was Flicka, his mate, who was more protective. But they figured she was taking care of her pup so thought no more about her.

Since Tusker wouldn't come for his food, Bob decided to get the car and shine its headlights down into the area where Tusker was barking. (It was dangerous for him to walk out around the coral rocks and grass at night.)

Suddenly, their African garden helper, Charo, came running from his mud hut. He was barefoot and had little on, but he knew the dog was in trouble and brought a big knife with him.

He went bravely to investigate, then came running back to report to the Williamses. "Tusker has a big cobra cornered," he told them. He ran to get a long stick and took it back, along with his knife.

Bob and Jean heard the "wap, wap" of Charo hitting something. Then he came out of the dark, carrying a cobra about a yard long, on his stick. It was still writhing but dead. They all praised the Lord that Tusker had kept the dangerous cobra away from their homes and enabled Charo to kill it.

The next day, they discovered that Flicka's throat and neck were swollen three times their normal size. They found drops of blood on the porch. So she must have found the snake first, after all, and tried to chase it away. But she had gotten drops of venom from the snake's fangs on her face. They took her to a veterinarian and he said that since she had lived that long she must be strong and had overcome the venom.

Then two weeks later, on a Sunday afternoon, Bob and Jean woke from their afternoon siesta or rest. (In most tropical countries, the intense heat makes it necessary for people to stay indoors in the afternoon and rest.)

They heard Tusker barking off somewhere. Jean went out in front of the house and found bright red drops of blood on the cement again. "Bob," she called, "come look at this."

"Looks as if one of the dogs is in trouble again," he said grimly. They circled the house and found

Flicka lying in the grass, her tongue out, her face bloody. She was barely breathing.

"Oh, Bob, she must have been bitten again!" Jean cried. "And she's in bad shape this time."

"And it sounds as if Tusker may have a snake cornered," he said. Tusker was about 100 yards away, barking excitedly. Bob grabbed a lead pipe nearby and ran to help.

"Be careful, Bob," Jean warned.

Sure enough, Tusker was dancing around and around a much larger cobra. The snake's head was up, swaying back and forth, trying to strike.

When Tusker saw Bob coming, he charged in, grabbed the snake in his teeth and shook it. At one point, he had its entire head in his mouth.

Bob moved forward carefully. The cobra's bite is deadly to a human being, he knew. Finally, he lunged and hit the snake on the head hard and it fell back dead.

Poor Flicka didn't survive this second attack. It was Sunday so the veterinarian's office was closed and he had left no emergency phone number. She died about 10 o'clock that night. Tusker started to swell, but they got him to the vet the next day and he recovered.

Bob and Jean praise God for their furry "guardian angels"—two brave dogs who were willing, if necessary, to give their lives to protect their masters.

Playful Water Clown

by Gloria A. Truitt

I know a little animal
  Who acts just like a clown.
He likes to climb up riverbanks,
  So he can slide back down.
He can turn a somersault . . .
  Roll over, swim, and dive,
And in the forest ponds and streams
  This animal will thrive.
His heavy coat of dark brown fur
  Protects him under water;
And there, he catches fish for food . . .
  Our clown, the *river otter!*

Starlight

A FICTION STORY by Delnora M. Erickson

"COME, STARLIGHT," Tom Shoemaker called to his pony as he opened the pasture gate.

The sleek gray pony trotted up to Tom and nuzzled his shoulder. Tom held out a couple of carrots and Starlight took them eagerly. "One of your favorite foods, huh, boy?" Tom said, grinning. He rubbed his pony's nose, then hopped on its back.

He and the pony had been friends for two years now. As they headed across the fields, Tom thought about how he had found Starlight in the pasture with a big tag on his neck that read, "Happy Tenth Birthday, Tom." And what a happy day that had been!

Today, however, Tom felt discouraged. His father had been ill since early summer. He had stayed several weeks in the hospital. Now all the family savings were gone.

The Shoemakers were Christians. Each day they prayed for help and healing for Dad. And Dad was much better. But today Mom had been worried about some big unpaid bills.

"We just don't have any money and the bills are overdue," she had said.

But what could Tom do? He had to go to school and was too young for regular work. His mom still had to stay home with Dad, and the twins were just babies.

On the way home, Tom noticed a strange car in the driveway. "I wonder who's visiting?" he said aloud. In the pasture, he slid off his pony and hurried to the house.

He stopped in the kitchen. His parents were talking to a man in the living room. The man was saying, "You name your price. That pony is just what I want for Dave."

Tom held his breath, waiting for his parents to answer. "Starlight belongs to Tom, Mr. Douglas," his father said. "We wouldn't sell him."

Tom sighed with relief.

"My son and I are renting the Beyer place," the man continued. "Dave is recovering from crippling arthritis. He's always wanted a pony. I hoped that moving here to the country and getting him one would get him off his crutches. But I can't force you to sell. If you change your minds, do let me know."

Tom turned and walked slowly back out to the pasture to think. Dave Douglas needed a pony and his parents needed the money.

That night, he talked to the Lord about Mr. Douglas'

offer. "Please, Lord, send the money we need some other way. You know I don't want to sell Starlight."

His parents didn't mention selling the pony, but Tom could see how concerned they were about their unpaid bills.

Three weeks later, Mr. Douglas returned and made a better offer for the pony. "I haven't been able to find one gentle enough for Dave to handle," he said.

This time Tom spoke up, "I don't like giving up Starlight, but I'll sell him to you. My parents need the money."

Mr. Douglas was delighted. "I'll be over tomorrow with the money and take the pony then," he said.

Tom got up earlier than usual the next day and took an apple out to his pony. Then he had a long ride before breakfast. "They'll be good to you," he told Starlight. "And I'll come and see you sometimes."

The pony nodded as if he understood.

"We'll make it up to you, Son," his father said that evening. "As soon as I'm able to work so there's money coming in, we'll get you another pony." But Tom was sure no other pony could take Starlight's place.

Two weeks went by. He missed his pony and decided to go over to the Douglases' place and visit him. When he rode up on his bike, a boy came to the door on crutches.

"Are you Tom?" the boy asked.

Tom nodded.

"Dad's going to send the pony back. He won't let me ride him."

Tom had a moment of panic. He knew the money had already been paid out on bills. "B-but, why?" he asked. "Starlight's a gentle pony."

"Well, he's not gentle when I try to ride him," Dave said, unhappily.

"May I see him?" Tom asked.

"Sure, he's in the pasture."

Tom heard a familiar whinny and turned to see Starlight standing by the fence. He was pawing the ground as he often did when he saw Tom near.

Tom pulled an apple from his pocket. Starlight reached over the fence and took it while Dave watched.

Tom prayed silently that God would show him how to help Dave. Then he turned to the boy on crutches. "I could come over every Saturday and help you and Starlight get acquainted," he offered.

"Why would you do that?" a man's voice asked from behind them.

Tom turned to Mr. Douglas. "Well, I believed that the Lord wanted Dave to have Starlight, so I'm sure He'd want me to help."

"We don't know anything about God," Mr. Douglas said, "but I'd appreciate your help for Dave's sake. He's been pretty disappointed."

"Then let's begin right now," Tom suggested.

Dave was willing so Tom put the bridle on Starlight and led him to the porch. The pony was trembling and shied away from Dave.

"Say, I know what's wrong with Starlight," Tom said. "The crutches are scaring him."

Tom held the pony and talked soothingly to him while Dave handed his crutches to his father and pulled himself into the saddle.

After the first uneasy moments, Dave seemed to relax and enjoy the ride. Twenty minutes later, Tom helped him dismount.

"That was fun!" Dave exclaimed.

"You're doing real well, son," Mr. Douglas said. "We sure appreciate your help, Tom."

From then on, after his chores were done each Saturday, Tom rode his bike over to the Douglases and helped Dave and Starlight get used to each other. Sometimes Dave would urge Tom to take a ride on Starlight himself, and it would be like old times again.

Tom had opportunities to talk to Dave about the Lord Jesus too. Dave, who was a year older than Tom, seemed interested and began to ask questions. Tom explained about sin in the world and how Jesus had come from heaven to take the punishment of man's sin so man could be free. He talked a lot about God's love too, and Dave listened.

One Saturday, Dave said, "Tom, I want the Lord Jesus to forgive my sins and live in my heart."

"That's great!" Tom said. "Why don't we both pray right now, and you can tell the Lord how you feel."

After that, Tom and Dave learned Bible verses during the week and quoted them to each other on Saturday. It was like a game, and Dave was learning more and more about God and His love.

A month went by. Winter was coming. Starlight was no longer afraid of Dave's crutches. He stood patiently and let Dave mount. One day when Tom arrived, Mr. Douglas met him first. "We don't need Starlight anymore," he said. "You can take him back."

Tom was stunned. "T-take him back?!" But would that mean they'd have to *buy* Starlight back, he wondered. He knew his father couldn't pay for the pony.

Just then Dave walked from the house and greeted Tom with his latest verse: "For we walk by faith, not by sight" (2 Cor. 5:7).

It suddenly hit Tom. "Dave, you're walking!" he cried.

Dave grinned. "Thanks for all your help, Tom. The Lord's given me the courage to walk alone. We're going back to the city, and I'll get back into school. But I'll sure miss you and Starlight."

"I'm giving Starlight to you, Tom," Mr. Douglas said. "We're so grateful that you were willing to give him up when Dave needed him.

"But I'm even more grateful that you told Dave about the Lord. Each Saturday evening Dave has shared with me what you two have talked about. Now I believe in Jesus as my Saviour too. We thank God every day for you, Tom."

Tom hated to say good-bye to Dave. But he left his bike for the time and rode Starlight home. As he turned and waved, Dave called after him, " 'And we know that all things work together for good to them that love God.' "

And Tom finished the verse with " 'to them who are the called according to His purpose' " (Rom. 8:28).

Cinder

A TRUE STORY by Gloria Truitt

JOHNNY TRUITT ran into the kitchen and skidded to a stop next to Mother who was washing dishes. He was quite out of breath. "Come quick!" he gasped. "See what we have on the sun porch!"

Dripping dishwater across the floor, Mother followed Johnny to the porch. "My goodness! What is that?" she asked. "A bear cub?"

Johnny's sister Laura stood by the door cuddling a whimpering ball of black, fluffy fur. Laura rubbed her cheek in the animal's soft fur and looked up at Mother with tears in her eyes. "Oh, Mom, of course she's not a bear! She's the cutest puppy in the world . . . and we want to keep her! Oh, please say *yes!*"

Johnny interrupted to explain how the man down the street could not find a home for her. She was the last of the litter and because no one would take her, the owner was going to have her destroyed in the morning.

"But what kind of a dog is she?" Mother asked. "I still think she looks like a bear!"

"Well," said Johnny, "the man told us she's half German shepherd and half black Labrador with a little terrier mixed in. But what's the difference? Isn't she a beauty?"

"I have to admit she's cute," Mother answered, "but I really don't think we need a dog, especially with school starting soon. I'd be left with all the work of training her."

Laura began to sob. "But if we give her back, the dog pound will put her to sleep. Then we'll be murderers!" she cried.

Mother hugged Laura and said, "We certainly can't let that happen, so we'll keep her for a few nights. Maybe we can find someone who will give her a good home."

"Yippee! Hooray!" shouted Johnny and Laura. Even the puppy wagged her tail as if to say, "Thank-you."

When Daddy came home from work, he was surprised to see the puppy. Like the children, he also thought she was adorable. The family decided to name the dog Cinderella because no one wanted her.

During the next few days, Johnny and Laura asked friends and neighbors if they wanted a puppy. The answer was always the same: "No."

Two weeks passed. One day Daddy spent a long time hammering and sawing in the basement. Finally he came upstairs dragging a huge dog house with a sign painted over its door. The sign said, *Cinder's House*. When the children read the sign, they yelled with joy. Daddy smiled as he set the house on the sun porch. "It looks as if she's found a home, so I guess we can't call her Cinderella anymore!" he said. "So I named her Cinder."

Not long after that the Truitts discovered that their darling, loving pup had one terrible habit. Whenever she was bored or left alone, Cinder would chew up anything she could get her teeth into. That included windowsills, floor tiles, shoes, and plants.

For instance, one afternoon Mother went into the kitchen to find that Cinder had knocked over and then eaten her prize African violet. The following Saturday, Daddy installed 20 yards of new carpeting on the sun porch. The next morning when Mother looked out onto the porch, all she saw was a towering mountain of spaghetti-like strands of yarn. Cinder had ripped up all the new carpeting!

"That does it!" Mother shouted. "Cinder has to go!"

"Go where?" Johnny wailed, as Laura cried and hugged Cinder.

"I don't know," Mother said angrily, "but I'm going to make every effort to find another home for her."

Johnny tried to fight back his tears as he ran to his bedroom saying, "If you give Cinder away, I'm going too!"

Daddy just kept shaking his head, not wanting to believe what had happened. Everyone knew that Mother was very angry. Father put his arm around her and said, "Let's talk about this in the kitchen.

Laura, you stay here on the porch for a while with Cinder."

Mother and Daddy discussed the problem and decided to give Cinder another chance. Daddy agreed to replace the carpeting if Cinder could sleep in the kitchen. Mother agreed to keep her violets in a different room.

All went well for about two weeks. Then one evening while the family was putting together a puzzle on the dining room table, Cinder wandered into the family room. She tore a big piece of leather off the Truitt's *brand-new* sofa.

Johnny saw the damage first. He took a pillow and placed it over the missing upholstery, so Mother would not see.

The next day, Mother hung her best sweater over the back of a dining room chair. An hour later she found it on the floor. "Oh, no, not again!" she cried as she poked her hand through the large hole that Cinder had chewed. Things were going from bad to worse!

That evening Laura and Johnny were playing with the train set in the family room when Mother came in to watch. She sat down on the sofa and suddenly the pillow fell over! "What's this?" she cried when she saw the torn upholstery. "Don't tell me! I already know!"

The children ran from the room, afraid to hear what Mother would say next. Cinder was afraid too, for she sneaked off to the kitchen and hid beneath the table. She knew she had done something very bad, and was in for a spanking.

Johnny and Laura cowered under the table while Mother and Daddy talked. "We simply can't afford to replace everything that dog destroys!" Mother cried. "Scolding doesn't help. Spanking her with a newspaper doesn't seem to either. And since we can't find someone who'll take her, I think we should call the dog pound."

Father sounded sad as he answered, "I know, but we've had her for almost four months. And the children have grown so attached to her. I know we'll break their hearts if we get rid of her. I remember how terrible I felt as a child when the police came and shot my dog."

Mother nodded. "And I remember having to give up a dog because my parents thought it was full of germs," she said.

Mother and Daddy decided to pray about Cinder. They were sure that God would help them to do the right thing. That night Johnny and Laura prayed too. They knew that only God could help solve the problem so that they could keep their pet.

The next day when Daddy came home from work, he cut some material from the back of the sofa and repaired the hole. It looked almost like new. Then the family sat down to discuss Cinder's future.

Daddy cleared his throat and, with a twinkle in his eye, explained that he and Mother had grown to love Cinder too. "We phoned the veterinarian," Daddy said. "He suggested that we keep a good supply of bones for Cinder to chew on. And whatever happens Mother and I decided, we will just make the best of it. After all, we can't get rid of a family member, can we?"

Laura and Johnny cheered, and Cinder thumped her tail happily against the table leg.

Everyone agreed that the Lord had answered their prayers through the vet's good advice. After all, wasn't love and concern for one of God's own creatures more important than material things?

After the Truitts decided to keep Cinder, they had only a few more chewing incidents. (One is told in "A Meatloaf Thanksgiving.") The Truitts gave Cinder large shank bones which seemed to satisfy her unusual appetite. These bones, along with humane discipline, restored harmony once again to the Truitt household. THE EDITOR

A Meatloaf Thanksgiving

A TRUE STORY by Gloria Truitt

ONE morning in late November, Johnny Truitt stood at the kitchen counter sniffing freshly baked pumpkin pies. "They sure smell good, Mama," he said. "I can't wait till tomorrow!"

Mother turned and smiled. "Just don't put a finger in any of those pies," she said.

Cinder, their half-grown, wooly black dog, thumped her tail from where she lay under the table. "And that goes for you too, Cinder!" Mother said, glancing under the table. "You get that hungry gleam out of your eyes."

Cinder had a terrible habit—at least she had had a terrible habit—of chewing anything she could get her teeth on. She had ruined many things in the house when she was a young pup.

A veterinarian had advised the family to give

51

Cinder large bones to gnaw on so she wouldn't chew more valuable things. For a long time now, Cinder hadn't chewed up anything she shouldn't.

Just then 10-year-old Laura came into the kitchen with a long face. "Grandma's on the phone and wants to talk to you, Mama," Laura said.

Mother hurried to the phone. When she came back, her face was as long as Laura's. "Grandma and Grandpa can't come tomorrow," she said. "They are having a bad snow storm."

Daddy came into the kitchen in time to hear what Mother said. "It will be a sad Thanksgiving without the folks," he said. "But wouldn't we rather have them safe than driving on those icy roads?"

Everyone agreed, but still it would not be the same without Grandma and Grandpa.

Mother glanced at the huge turkey thawing on the kitchen counter. "What a shame," she said, sighing. "That bird is much too big for only four people."

"And those pies!" Daddy exclaimed. "One would have been plenty!" After a moment, he added. "Wait a minute! I have an idea! Besides giving thanks to the Lord for all the good things He gives us, shouldn't Thanksgiving be a special time for sharing?"

"Why, yes!" cried Laura.

"But who could we share our Thanksgiving dinner with?" Johnny asked.

"Think hard," Mother said. "We must know someone who spends Thanksgiving alone."

One by one the family phoned the people they knew. Each answer was the same—"Thank-you very much, but we've already made plans for dinner tomorrow."

Just when Mother and Daddy were about to give up, Johnny blurted out, "What about the Olsons who go to our church and live in the senior citizens' home? Even if we don't know them well, we could still ask them to dinner, couldn't we? They don't have any family, and they always look lonely."

"That's a wonderful suggestion, Johnny," Mother said, smiling. She phoned the Olsons and when she hung up, told the family, "It's all set. The Olsons are delighted. They said they would be here at 1 o'clock tomorrow afternoon."

"Whoopee! Hooray!" the family cheered. Even Cinder barked happily as if to say, "I'm glad we're having special company to share our Thanksgiving."

Early the next morning, Mother stuffed the turkey and popped it into the oven. While the turkey was roasting, Laura and Johnny helped Mother set the dining room table. At last the turkey was done, and Mother took it out of the oven. How wonderful it looked—golden brown, juicy, and bursting with delicious dressing!

Just then Daddy called from the family room. "If you're not too busy, dear, come and see the new freight car we've added to the train set!"

Mother left the turkey on the counter and joined the family. Minutes later, she glanced at her watch. "Oh, my!" she said. "It's almost 1 o'clock. The Olsons will be here soon, and I don't have the rolls ready!"

Mother dashed back to the kitchen, but stopped

dead in the doorway. An awful sight met her eyes! There on the floor was the Thanksgiving turkey. It had been chewed all over. Chunks of stuffing lay scattered among the pieces of torn meat. Cinder sat contentedly in the corner, wagging her tail.

"Cinder!" Mother screamed. "How could you! You bad dog!" Then she called to the family, "Come quickly! Something terrible has happened!"

Daddy and the children almost fell over each other, trying to get into the kitchen to see what was wrong. For a moment they were too stunned to speak. "Our turkey is ruined!" Laura wailed.

Mother looked as if she was about to cry. Daddy put his arm around her and said quietly, "Thanksgiving is more than a turkey. Come on, we'll think of something." He opened the refrigerator and took out a package of ground beef. "Here we go," he said. "We'll have a meat loaf Thanksgiving."

Then Daddy got a rolled up newspaper and took Cinder out of the kitchen.

When the doorbell rang, Daddy greeted the Olsons. Mother prepared the meat loaf, while everyone else visited. Some time later, after everyone had been seated at the table, Daddy prayed. He thanked the Lord for His gift of salvation, for the food, and for loving friendships. Then Mother told the Olsons what had happened to the turkey.

Throughout dinner, everyone talked happily. When the meal was over, the family took the Olsons into the family room to show them the train set. Too soon, the day was over and it was time for the Olsons to leave. Mrs. Olson grasped Mother's hand. "Thank-you for a wonderful Thanksgiving Day—and a delicious meal!" she said.

A warm smile lit up Mr. Olson's face, as he added, "—And that meat loaf was the best tasting *turkey* we've ever had!"

Just then Cinder walked out from behind a chair, looking rather satisfied in spite of her spanking. Johnny looked at the dog and laughed. "I think Cinder enjoyed her dinner too!" Everyone laughed then—even Mother!

The Lonesome Frog

by Gloria A. Truitt

Once I found a happy frog
   Living wild and free.
I put him in an earth-filled bowl
   And brought him home with me.
I fed him crawling bugs each day . . .
   (They had to be alive!)
But even though he ate those bugs,
   He didn't seem to thrive.
His little body seemed to shrink . . .
   His legs grew thin and weak . . .
And then his hearty, singing *croak*
   Became a creaky *squeak!*
One day I took him back to live
   With all the other frogs,
And once again he's happy with
   His wife and polliwogs!

Adventure on Big Pine Island

A FICTION STORY by Craig Massey

"MARK, just what are you going to do with those pigeons at our picnic?" Tom Nichols asked as he peered at the grey-blue birds in the small basket Mark Johnson was carrying.

"I'm taking them on a training flight," Mark said. "When we get to Big Pine Island, I'll let them go and they'll fly home. Next week my dad is going to take them farther out on the lake when he goes fishing. Some day I'll enter them in a pigeon race."

Tom laughed. "You mean to tell me that those silly-looking bundles of feathers can find their way home from Big Pine Island? Why, that's 15 miles from here. At least half that distance is over water." Tom was scornful.

"Tom, these aren't ordinary pigeons. They're homing pigeons," Mark tried to explain. "God has given them a special instinct. They can find their way home from great distances—over hundreds of miles."

"Aw, you're crazy," Tom said. "I'll never believe they can find their way home from Big Pine."

"Look in the *World Book* sometime," Mark explained. "It tells about homing pigeons and how they were used to carry messages in wartime. I've read in other books too, how the soldiers took them to the battlelines. When they had to send a message to the rear, they'd write a coded message on a small piece of paper and put it in a tube, and fasten it to the pigeon's leg.

"After the pigeon was released, it would fly back with the message. One pigeon in World War I, named Cher Ami, saved the lives of many men who were trapped by gunfire."

"Well, that doesn't mean yours can do that!" Tom sounded jealous now. But Mark didn't argue. The two boys were in club together at church and had met on their way to a club picnic. Mark knew that Tom wasn't a Christian. He kept hoping Tom would accept Jesus as his Saviour, so he tried not to fight when Tom gave him a bad time.

At church, they met Mr. Falls, their club leader, and the rest of the boys. "There they are," Mr. Falls called as Tom and Mark walked up. "I guess we're all here now. Climb into the van, fellows. We'll drive down to the dock. I have the boat all ready."

In no time at all nine fellows and Mr. Falls were aboard a sleek, fiberglass inboard motor boat, zipping out into Cranberry Lake. It was a hot day and the cold spray hitting them felt good. But when Mark saw it splashing the pigeon basket, he threw his wind breaker over it for protection.

Tom noticed. "Do you still think those old pigeons will get back home?" he demanded. "Look, the shoreline's already almost out of sight."

Mark simply said, "Wait and see."

Tom had once told him that his dad didn't believe in God because no one could see Him. Mark realized that Tom probably didn't believe in anything he couldn't see either. Though it seemed hopeless, Mark prayed that somehow Tom would come to realize that there was a God who loved him, and would receive the Lord Jesus Christ as his Saviour.

At last the boat glided up to the sandy shore of Big Pine Island, and the guys tumbled out. The Island was low, but the beach was just right for games and swimming. A grove of tall pine trees gave the island its name.

Mark unloaded the pigeons and Tom asked, "Well, are you going to turn them loose now?"

"I think I'll wait till we start home. Then we can see if they beat us," Mark answered.

"Aw, you're afraid to let them go," Tom scoffed. "You know they can't make it!"

"Tom, I think you're going to be in for a surprise," Mr. Falls said, after overhearing Tom's remark. "Those pigeons *will* probably beat us home if Mark lets them go just as we leave."

The early part of the afternoon was spent, swimming and playing games on the beach. At about 3

P.M., Mr. Falls suggested that they explore the other end of the island.

A glad shout greeted his suggestion, and soon they were hiking along the beach.

An hour later, Mr. Falls said, "Look at those rain clouds. We'd better head back to our stuff and the boat. Storms on the lake can be pretty bad."

The boys started off running. Soon a strong wind carrying rain hit them and high waves began breaking over the beach, slowing them down.

"Wow, what a ride we're going to have on the way back," Bryan Clark shouted over the wind.

"M-maybe we should stay on the island till the storm is over," Tom suggested. Mark glanced over at Tom and saw fear on his face.

"We can't," Mr. Falls said. "In a bad storm waves can sweep right over this low island."

When they reached their picnic site, a shock awaited them. "The boat's gone!" Billy Bender yelled.

"We're in trouble for sure, now," Mark said.

"I see it. Way out there, Mr. Falls," Bryan said.

Sure enough, the red speedboat was drifting farther and farther away from the island. The wind and waves had broken the mooring rope.

"Now what do we do?" Tom moaned.

"There's not much we can do except hope somebody spots our boat and comes out to get us," Jack Crane said.

"Don't forget that we have a heavenly Father, boys. He's looking out for us all the time," Mr. Falls reminded them.

"Mr. Falls, I know what we can do," Mark said just then. "I still have my pigeons. We can write out messages, then tie them to the pigeons' legs and let them fly back home for help."

"I forgot your pigeons," Mr. Falls said. "That might work."

"Hey, neat idea!" Billy agreed.

"Aw, you and your old pigeons!" Tom said. "How can they fly eight miles across the lake in this wind?"

"I'm sure they can make it," Mark said. "It will be good experience for them."

"I have a piece of paper," Mr. Falls said. "Does anyone have a pencil?"

"I have," Bryan answered, fishing in his pocket.

Mr. Falls took it and wrote two messages exactly alike. They read, "Lost our boat. Ten of us stranded on Big Pine Island. Send help right away. Storm is bad!"

Mark tied the notes on the pigeons with a piece of strong thread that he pulled from his jeans.

"Before we let the pigeons go, let's pray," Mr. Falls suggested. Then he asked the Lord to help the pigeons get through the storm and prayed that God would take care of each member of the group.

Afterward, Mark loosed the birds in the driving rain. Up and up they went, bucking the wind. They circled higher and higher till the boys lost sight of them in the clouds and rain.

An hour passed and still the storm tore over the island. The group huddled together under the pines, trying to keep warm. Tom was very quiet while the

other boys joked and told ghost stories. Mark prayed silently that the pigeons would reach home and that Mom and Dad would see the messages.

It was almost dark when suddenly Mr. Falls called out, "Look, lights on the lake. It looks like a boat heading for the island!" They all jumped up and ran to the beach, waving and yelling.

A large motor boat bounded up to the beach through the high waves and a man splashed overboard with a rope. "Dad!" Mark exclaimed with delight.

"You OK?" his father called out.

"We sure are!" Mr. Falls answered. "But we're glad to see you."

The boys crowded around, yelling and talking at once as the men helped them aboard one at a time.

When they were on their way again, Mr. Johnson said, "Mark, your pigeons reached home at the same time. I just happened to be out in the yard getting things in out of the rain. I saw the pigeons flying in and noticed the messages on their legs. I contacted Mr. Alstair and he lent us his boat to come out and pick you up."

The ride home through the choppy waves was exciting, but Mark hardly noticed as Tom leaned over and said, "I still can't understand how your pigeons managed to find their way home!"

"Tom," Mark said, "there are some things we can't understand. We just have to believe them anyway. You didn't believe the pigeons could make it until they proved themselves. Well, it's the same way with accepting the Lord Jesus as Saviour. Maybe you can't see Him, but if you receive Him as your Saviour, He will prove Himself to you."

This time Tom didn't scoff. He just looked away and nodded. Mark barely caught his words as the wind almost blew them away. "Yes, I think I see what you mean—now."

Five Creatures God Used

TRUE STORIES by Joseph T. Larson

1. When evangelist George Whitefield preached in Philadelphia many years ago, one man wanted to see the evangelist. But he didn't want to hear the Gospel. He climbed a tree and put a finger in each ear.

A fly landed on his nose and kept him busy swinging at it. As Whitefield preached, the man heard the message and was convicted of his sin. He slid down the tree and pushed through the crowd to receive Christ as his Saviour.

2. Some years ago I talked with an elderly man who had come from Greece. He told me that, as a boy, he had run away to Turkey from his home in Greece. He was afraid of the police and the people and dared not show himself. He lived under a railroad viaduct for six days.

During those six days, a strange but friendly dog brought him loaves of bread. How the dog managed each day, the boy could not understand. But he was kept from starvation by the dog.

He was spared by God, he told me, so he could become a Christian at my Gospel meetings in Iowa!

Certainly "God moves in a mysterious way His wonders to perform!" as William Cowper said.

3. Years ago I knew a preacher, the Rev. William Kelly. When he was a boy he lived in Missouri. Some Saturday nights he went dancing. Other Saturdays he went to a church to attend revival meetings. One Saturday night he sat on his saddle horse, undecided about where to go. He said to himself, "I guess I'll let the horse decide it."

The horse took him to the church, where he heard a powerful sermon. He went forward to receive Christ as his personal Saviour. Later he was called into the Gospel ministry, and served the Lord for 54 years.

4. I heard of a fox terrier that followed his mistress to church each Sunday. When the woman died, her husband noticed that the dog went somewhere every Sunday morning. He followed the dog one Sunday and saw him enter the church.

The dog's loyalty touched the man's heart. The man began attending church and also received Christ.

5. About 200 years ago David Brainerd, the missionary to the forest Indians, was caught in a severe storm. He found a shelter in the hollow of a big log. In the log, he prayed for the salvation of the Indians. He also asked God to take care of his needs.

When mealtime came, he saw a squirrel approaching. The chattering animal dropped some nuts nearby and left. Brainerd ate them, as well as others the squirrel brought him during two more stormy days.

How wonderful are God's ways!

A Story of the Buffalo

by Gloria A. Truitt

Before Columbus sailed the seas,
   Many years ago,
Our western plains were grazing grounds
   For herds of buffalo.
One herd could total millions,
   So imagine, if you can,
How many buffalo there were
   Before the *rush* began.
The Indians were very smart,
   And hunted only those
Which they could use for moccasins,
   Their food, and winter clothes.

But then the white men came along
  To cultivate this plain,
And put up fences for their steers
  And planted fields of grain.
They stretched a track across the land
  To guide the *iron horse,*
And meanwhile the great buffalos
  Were slaughtered in the course.
The saddened Indians looked on
  With tears at what remained,
For now the white men ruled where once
  The buffalo had reigned.
A lonely few now roamed the west . . .
  They'd all but disappeared!
Too soon they would become extinct,
  A group of people feared.
These people asked the government
  To save the buffalo,
And now in national parks and zoos
  We watch their numbers grow.
Across the plains, in game preserves,
  Large herds can safely roam . . .
And once again this king of beasts
  Can call our land his home!

"I'll Never Forgive Him!"

A TRUE STORY by Irene Aiken

FOR two years, 11-year-old Lloyd Nixon and his chubby black dog, Butch, had played games and climbed trees together. Yes, Butch had climbed too—with help from Lloyd. On school days, Butch had run beside Lloyd's bike—all the way to school.

Now a young policeman stood at the Nixon's door with an official notice. The notice said that Lloyd must either find another home for his dog—outside the city limits—or have Butch destroyed!

"Son, I'm awfully sorry," the young police officer said, after handing the notice to Lloyd's mother. "I know how you feel. I used to have a dog myself. But your dog bit the paper boy, and the dog has to be done away with. Our city law says so!" The young man sighed when he saw Lloyd's tears.

"But I could tie him up—or we could build a fence

or—" Lloyd said, wiping at the tears on his face. He turned to look at his mother behind him, but she shook her head sadly. He knew that it was simply no use!

"I'm afraid it's too late for that now," she said. "I'm sorry, honey." Mother put her arms around Lloyd. "But we can run an ad in the newspaper. We'll find a good home for Butch with a farmer. You'll see."

Lloyd flung himself away from his mother and gathered Butch into his arms. He hugged his dog as if he would never let him go. He hardly heard the policeman say as he turned to leave, "You have a week, Ma'am, and I *am* sorry."

At supper, Lloyd sat without eating. He didn't feel at all hungry. His brother and sister talked and argued as usual, but he didn't even notice. However, when his sister, Doris, mentioned Butch, he perked up his ears.

"That paper boy pulled a knife on Butch one day. I saw him! He's a mean boy—he is!" she exclaimed, angrily.

Lloyd heard her—and wiped at his face. How dare that boy threaten Butch and then blame the dog for trying to get even with him! Butch was simply protecting his family. How could a dog know that the paper boy was not an enemy!

"I'll never forgive him for doing this to Butch and me!" Lloyd said, his heart full of sorrow and anger. He looked at Doris a long minute. She was telling the truth! Suppose he told the policeman about the boy's knife?

But when he suggested it, his brother spoke from

the lofty wisdom of 13 years. "It wouldn't do any good to try to change things. Once the law gets going, you can't fight it. You know that!"

And to Lloyd's horror, the next morning the ad appeared in the paper: "Boy loves dog so much that he wants to give him away, free, to a good home in the country, away from city streets." Their phone number was listed too, but Lloyd could hardly read it for the tears in his eyes.

He put the paper down and got ready for school, feeling numb. He could hear Butch whining outside the back door where he was fastened by his leash to the clothesline.

Butch was used to freedom. The town was small, and had no leash law. Many dogs ran up and down the streets. But not Butch. He would never be free to run in this town again!

Lloyd went off to school, still wiping at his face. When he came home that afternoon, he saw, to his horror, that Butch's leash was hanging empty! The small doghouse was missing too! Lloyd stood there, shocked. Mother had given his dog away this very day!

"Dear, a nice man called, then came for Butch. Your dog now has a new home 10 miles out in the country." Mother sounded hoarse as if maybe she had been crying too. "Isn't that wonderful?"

"It's not wonderful. It's horrible—and stupid. And I hate you too. I'll never see my dog again!" Lloyd said, and ran to his room. He crawled under his bed and rolled up in a ball of misery, the way he had when he was very small. He hated the whole world—even God.

Why *had* God let this happen to him? Hadn't he gone to Sunday School all his life and been a good boy? Surely God could have figured out some way to stop this terrible thing.

Then he thought about that mean paper boy—and was filled to the brim with hate for him. It was all his fault.

"Maybe I can get even with him for this!" Lloyd thought. And quickly he came out from under his bed. At that moment he heard Mother calling him. "There's somebody here to see you."

He went to the front door, and who should be standing there but the hated paper boy! Lloyd gasped.

"I'm sorry about the dog," the boy said. "Really I am. He got to chasing me, and I had to show him my knife, so he'd stop nipping at my heels as I rode by on my bike. Then one morning, I fell off the bike, and he bit me. My folks took me to the doctor, and they set out to get rid of your dog. They both hate dogs. I've never had a pet in my life."

But Lloyd wasn't about to forgive this enemy who was as old as Carl, his brother. "You made that up about Butch nipping your heels," Lloyd shouted. "You've been mean to him—and he was just being mean back."

"Look, kid, I said I was sorry. What else can I do?" the boy said, turning away. "You're lucky—at least you had a dog—and had him a long time."

Mother had been standing nearby. When the paper boy left, she closed the door and said quietly to Lloyd, "Come with me. I have something for you to read."

She led the way to the living room and took down her Bible. Quickly, she found a verse and showed it to Lloyd. He knew it already! "And be ye kind one to another, tenderhearted, forgiving one another, even as God for Christ's sake hath forgiven you" (Eph. 4:32). Lloyd had memorized that verse in Sunday School.

Tears rolled down his face once more. But this time they were tears of sorrow over his own anger and hate. God would have to help him forgive the paper boy—that poor boy who had never owned a dog in his life!

He was thinking some deep and troubled thoughts when the phone rang. Mother answered it, then smiled as she listened. When she hung up, she said, "Lloyd, that was the man who adopted Butch.

"He said that Butch is very happy. He is playing in the green clover and loves it. He even chased and nearly caught a rabbit! Their little boy is thrilled to have Butch. He's never had a dog before. The man said to tell you, God bless you."

Lloyd had one more long cry then in his mother's arms. It was hard to lose his dog, but he was glad another boy could enjoy Butch. Finally, when he could speak again, he said, "I'll tell the paper boy that I'm sorry, next time I see him."

Miss Muskrat Builds a House

by Gloria A. Truitt

Wouldn't it be fun to watch
   Miss Muskrat build her house?
Although she's called a rodent, she's
   Quite different from a mouse.
Miss Muskrat likes to live in streams,
   A pond, or tiny lake,
And there, right in the middle,
   A fine castle she will make.
She'll build a pile of reeds and grass. . .
   (It could be five feet high!)
And sometimes she'll use cattails if
   They're on the banks nearby.
Inside her castle she'll keep snug
   And warm in her fur coat,
And there she'll live quite safe from harm
   Surrounded by a moat!

A Sheep Called Sheba

told by Tommy Houvenagle, 12
written by Shirley Houvenagle

ONE rainy April Sunday my grandmother called me on the phone. She said a friend of hers had a female orphaned lamb to give away. If I wanted it, she would drive out and get it for me.

Dressing as fast as I could, I filled a pop bottle half full of milk and put on it the long black nipple we use for feeding lambs. I thought the lamb might need food right away, especially if it was cold and weak.

Dad took me right over to Grammy's. On the way there I tried to picture the new lamb. I had once thought all sheep looked alike. But now I was aware that they were as different from each other as people are. I wished I had asked whether it was a black- or white-faced sheep. Not that it really mattered that much.

The minute the car stopped rolling, I ran for Gram-

my's back door. I swung it open and raced in. Then I stopped and stared. Instead of the woolly-looking baby I had expected, there, in a box of straw, stood the strangest looking creature. She looked as if she had just stepped from the pages of a Dr. Seuss book!

Her face was long and narrow. Her black eyes were huge. She had a black dot beside each eye. She didn't appear to have any ears at all. A wide black stripe ran down each leg. Her underside was black but the rest of her body was white with reddish-brown spots across the back.

"What is it?" I gasped.

Grammy laughed and explained that the lamb was an Asiatic Mountain sheep of Tibetan origin. Her owners had imported a male and female several years ago to eat weeds in their pastures.

Because these sheep were so hardy, their owners seldom paid much attention to them. They had noticed, however, that one mother had a baby which had died two weeks earlier. But they didn't know she had actually had twins until they saw this second lamb. They were afraid the mother would neglect it too, so they decided to give it away.

I cuddled the odd-looking lamb in my arms. She nestled against me with wide, frightened eyes as I stroked her silky hair. However, she pulled away when I pried her mouth open and put the nipple between her teeth. It was two days before she started sucking.

The third day she became very ill from her new diet. Apparently cow's milk was too rich for her. I thought for sure she'd die.

Our family had a special prayer meeting for the sick lamb. We all asked God to give us the wisdom to raise her, if it was His will that she live.

The next day a neighbor lady invited my mother to coffee. She told mother that sometimes beaten raw eggs mixed with milk would settle stomach problems in baby animals. We tried it and it worked!

The lamb sure looked funny sitting on Mother's lap, being spoonfed. Egg dribbled down her chin as she struggled to free herself. I guess she didn't care for the taste, but a day later she was better.

Because she had been sick and was so young, she ate every two hours, day and night. While I was at school, mother fed her. At night I slept in a sleeping bag in the living room with an alarm clock nearby. That way I could get up without disturbing the rest of the family.

Meanwhile, I was searching for a name that was just right for the lamb. I went over some Bible names and came to Bathsheba. It fit! Soon we were calling her just "Sheba."

Sheba stayed in a playpen in the furnace room until she was a month old. By that time she was leaping over the side as fast as I could put her back in. When Dad caught her nibbling on some of his technical magazines, he said she had to move.

The only place available was the hay shed, with about 100 bales stacked in one end. But Sheba didn't mind. In fact, she loved it!

One morning when I went out to give her the bottle, I couldn't find her. Then I heard a bleat above my head and looked up on the bales of hay. There she stood, poised and peering down like an old owl. Without any warning, she sailed off the bales and landed at my feet. Was I shook up!

A day or two later I took her to school to show her off. My teacher took one look at her and said, "She's a goat!" My next school assignment was to find some information on Sheba's ancestors and give a report.

In my research, I discovered that Asiatic Mountain sheep are a lot like Rocky Mountain goats. Now I knew why she climbed and jumped. These activities were inborn.

In spite of the fact that we all played with her and laughed at her funny antics, Sheba was lonely. She didn't care for the other sheep and they didn't like her. She mostly just followed me around like a dog.

One day a stray puppy came to live with us. We had no other place for the pup, so we put her in the shed with Sheba. Soon the pup and lamb were merry friends. Sheba baaed constantly if "Biscuit," as we named the pup, wasn't with her. They made a strange looking pair, roughing around together.

After Sheba came to live with us, I got to thinking about all the strange and interesting animals God has made. Imagine Him making an animal like Sheba, then lending her to me!

A Sackful of Kittens

A TRUE STORY by Irene Aiken

AUNTY MAUD's kitchen smelled delicious that Saturday morning. I was helping my cousin Marie set the table for breakfast when I glanced out of the window in time to see Uncle Nash hurry around the corner of the house. He was carrying a sack full of something that was wriggling.

Marie saw him too, and began screaming as if someone had stuck her with a knife. "Oh, no, Daddy. No!" she yelled and dived for the back door.

"What in the world?" I gasped and saw Aunt Maud frowning. I ran out after Marie to see what was going on. She was still yelling. She had caught her father and was pulling on the sack he carried and screaming louder than ever. "You're *not* going to drown my kittens! You're not! You're not!"

I still remember how the wet grass soaked my

sneakers as I ran. The air was sweet from the smell of the huge honeysuckle vine all down the fence. Tears streamed down my face.

Samantha, the mama cat, had just had two kittens over a month ago. They were darlings! Marie and I had spent most of yesterday carrying them up and down nearby streets, trying to give them away. Nobody had wanted them. A newspaper ad had brought no replies.

I had stayed overnight with my cousin. She and I really enjoyed each other. She was a year older, imaginative, and fun. Both of us had blonde curly hair and hazel eyes—real kinfolk. But we lived two miles apart so we only got to see each other on weekends.

Marie pleaded with her father for the kittens and I stood there beside her with my heart clear down in my sneakers. I so much wanted one of the kittens myself. But my father was allergic to all animals with fur. I had fallen in love with the black and white kitten and had named him Tom. The other kitten was grayish. I felt as Marie did that it would be murder to drown them.

But Uncle Nash was trying to explain. "If you have kittens you can't give away, you take them down to the brook in a sack. It's a quick, merciful way for them to die. Already your mama cat is making you another litter of kittens. We simply can't keep them all, Marie. Be sensible! I was trying to do this before you knew about it. I know it makes you sad."

Marie still clung to the sack, trying to pull it from her father's hand. She was sobbing wildly.

"Now, Marie," her father said, "stop that this minute. You hear me? You're 12 years old. Too big for this kind of behavior."

"But, Daddy, couldn't we just give Samantha away and keep the kittens?" Marie pleaded, still weeping.

"No, we can't. Samantha is a good mouser. She keeps the mice out of the chicken feed. You know that, Marie." (My aunt and uncle raised chickens and sold eggs.)

"All right. All right, Daddy. But please give us one more day. Renie and I will find homes for them both, won't we?" she asked, whirling around to me.

"Oh, yes," I said. "We'll walk until we find homes for them." I drew a deep breath of relief when Uncle Nash gave Marie the wriggling sack. I had been praying silently that he would as I stood there.

"OK, you have one day," Uncle Nash said. "If you fail, I'll do this job tonight while you're asleep. I mean it, Marie. I don't like to do it anymore than you, but I know what I have to do."

Marie and I ate breakfast faster than I ever had before or since. Then we set out again, each of us with a kitten in our arms. I couldn't believe it when Marie said, "Daddy does this every time Samantha has kittens. He's mean!"

"My father said yours ought to get Samantha neutered," I told her. "Then she wouldn't have anymore kittens. Why don't grown-ups like kittens, I wonder?"

As we walked, I prayed again to the Saviour I loved and trusted. I knew He cared about kittens even if others didn't.

But it was the same as it had been the day before. Nobody wanted a kitten.

Our feet hurt so badly that we sat down on a curb to talk about what to do next. A few seconds later, we heard snoring and jumped nervously.

I turned and looked at the old abandoned house behind us. Its yard was overgrown with weeds and once-treasured flowers. We saw a man—obviously a hobo—lying on the old front porch, asleep.

Marie stood up. The look on her face said we'd better move on. But just then the hobo awakened and sat up. He looked at us with merry eyes. "Say, lemme see your kittens," he called. "I like cats." He yawned widely as we walked over to him. Marie held out her gray kitten to him.

"Well now, that's a fine cat," he said, smoothing the fur on the kitten's head and chin. The kitten began purring at once, and Marie began her often repeated speech, ending with "We'll give him to you, sir."

"Well, now, I think that would be nice. He would just fit into my big old pocket here. He can ride along with his head sticking out," the man said. "See?"

I saw that he wore a button on his lapel that said, "Jesus Saves," and I was sure that God was in this.

So we walked on with only my black and white Tom. Looking back, we saw the hobo walking toward the railroad with the gray kitten's head poking out of the old jacket pocket. I felt better now, but still we had to find a home for Tom or he'd die this very night!

We realized by now that we'd come so far across town that we were closer to my home than Marie's.

"Let's stop by my house and have a rest and cool drink," I suggested.

At the edge of our yard, we stopped. I couldn't take Tom inside. So we opened a small doorway to a crawl space under the house and put him there. Then we closed the door. He'd be safe and could rest while we rested.

Of course we had to explain to mother why we had walked across town. I even told her about praying and that I was sure God had one more "kitten" person waiting for us somewhere.

Mother looked at me oddly, then wiped her eyes. A little later she was on the phone, talking seriously to someone.

When she came back to the table where Marie and I were drinking Kool-Aid, she sat down and smiled. "That was your dad," she said. "I have good news for you. We are going to work it out so you can keep the kitten if you want to. But you'll have to fix it a house outdoors, like a doghouse. It must absolutely never come inside, OK?"

"Oh-h-h," was all I could say. I ran outside, my feet no longer tired, to tell Tom about the new deal. When Marie joined me, I said, "You phone your parents and tell them you're going to help me build a cat house this afternoon."

"But it's too big a job for kids like us!" she said, frowning.

I shook my head. Nothing was too big a job for me today. I had my kitten. If she didn't want to help me, I'd build it myself. "There's a lot of scrap lumber in the garage, also nails and hammers. Let's get started," I said.

"Oh, all right," she said. I knew that she was recalling the sack and her father's threat.

"You know what?" I said. "God did it. I prayed about the kittens." Seeing her wide-eyed disbelief, I repeated, "He did so. I know He did."

It was the very first time I had ever prayed and received such a quick answer. Gratitude and love for the Lord swelled in my chest as I picked up Tom and rubbed my face in his soft fur.

Arthur Aardvark
by Gloria A. Truitt

My friend called Arthur Aardvark
   Lives in the city zoo.
He traveled from far Africa,
   A town called Bandundu.*
His claws are shaped like chisels, and
   His sticky tongue is long.
He burrows with his tapered tail,
   Which really is quite strong.
For breakfast, lunch, and dinner
   His favorite food is ants!
He's not a vegetarian
   Like mammals which chew plants.
If we were asked to trade our meals,
   I don't know what we'd do,
For surely I'd not eat those ants . . .
   Nor would he eat Mom's stew!

---

*Bandundu is an actual town in Africa located in the Republic of
Zaire. There, and in the surrounding area, anteaters live in abun-
dance.

A Whale Out of Water

by Elsie M. Milligan

The incident about the baby whale in this story is true. It inspired the author to make up the rest of the story about a boy she named Jimmy Parsons.

THE EDITOR

"MOMMY, Mommy," called nine-year-old Jimmy Parsons excitedly as he dashed in from morning school. "There's a whale on the beach! Please, can I go and see it?"

"A whale!" exclaimed Mrs. Parsons. "Do you mean a dead one washed ashore?"

"No, Mom, it's alive, and it's a baby one. It's stuck in the sand."

"Well, it's nearly lunchtime, but we'll both go and see it right now," said his mother.

As they hurried down to the beach—Fish Hoek Bay

in South Africa—Jimmy explained what had happened. "All the boys were talking about it at school," he said. "The tide went out and left the whale out of water, stuck in the sand. They're afraid it'll die in the hot sun."

When they reached the nearby seashore, sure enough, there was a baby whale, lying in the golden sand. Crowds of people milled around, looking at it.

"Oh dear," said Jimmy's mother. "I'm afraid the poor little thing hasn't a hope in this hot sun. I wonder where its mother is?"

Just then the beach attendant passed by and heard what she said. He stopped and told them, "The mother is out there in the bay. She's raging back and forth in a terrible state because she can't come in and rescue her child."

"It looks quite big to me," said Jimmy, "not like a baby whale."

"We just had a marine expert here," the attendant answered. "He said it's a three-month-old and weighs about two tons."

"Some baby!" Jimmy exclaimed. "But will it die?"

"We're going to do all we can to save it, but I doubt if we'll succeed. The tide doesn't come in again till late this afternoon. We'll try to refloat it then. Meantime we'll pour sea water over it to keep it damp and cool."

Jimmy joined a group of boys right near the little whale. He put out his hand and stroked its shiny black back. He watched with interest as men came and laid wet sacks all over the whale. Then they brought large hoses to the beach and sprayed sea water over the sacks.

To Jimmy's great joy, he was allowed to hold one of the hoses for a few minutes. But then his mother called him home to eat.

As soon as possible, Jimmy was back at the beach again. There were even more people there now, all waiting anxiously for the tide to turn. Meantime the watering went on. The little whale showed no signs of life. Many people feared it was dead.

At long last the tide began to come in. Slowly, slowly, the breakers came nearer. A loud cheer broke from the crowd when the first wave went over the young whale. They hoped to see him float. But, alas, he didn't move. More waves came and broke over him till he was almost covered with water.

"Oh dear, he's dead!" cried Jimmy.

"No," said the attendant, "he's stuck too deep in the sand to move."

Just then two skin divers arrived. They dove down on each side of the whale and scooped out the sand under him. Then they got a strong canvas sheet and rolled it under the whale. Many willing hands helped them with this difficult job.

A row of men took hold of the canvas on each side. As each wave broke over them they heaved forward in a mighty effort to release the little whale.

Again and again they tried. At last a huge wave broke over them. As it receded they gave one more big heave. Lo and behold, the young whale rose up and out of the sand. Nobody breathed.

Suddenly, a feeble little spurt of water shot up from the whale. The crowd roared.

"He's alive! He's saved!" shouted Jimmy.

The next minute the whale gathered all his remaining strength and shot out into the bay. Full speed ahead he went till he joined his anxious mother. Together, they sped out to sea, amidst the claps, cheers, and shouts of hundreds of happy people.

What a story Jimmy had to tell his father when he got home! "And I helped save him because I squirted water on him," he added triumphantly.

Later, at bedtime, Jimmy's daddy said, "It's easy to see what happened to that young whale today. I guess his mother warned him not to swim inshore, but he didn't listen. When she called him, he just kept going. So he very nearly lost his life. Wasn't that it, Jimmy?"

"Yes, Daddy, I expect it was like that," Jimmy said squirming uneasily, "like—like me sometimes."

"Like all of us, Son," said Mr. Parsons. "Most of us are slow to listen to God's warnings. Did you know, Jimmy, that there is a verse in the Bible that says, 'But he who listens to Me shall live securely' (Prov. 1:33, NASB). It's a wise boy who listens to God's Word and obeys it. In fact, we can all learn a lesson from the whale's adventure today."

My Pet Turtle

by Gloria A. Truitt

My little pet turtle
Could ne'er jump a hurdle . . .
  His legs are nonsensically short.
He couldn't win races
Nor run baseball bases,
  Yet he's quite a diligent sport.
Though he acts lackadaisy
He's surely not lazy . . .
  (He carries his house everywhere!)
Round and round he will stroll
In his pretty glass bowl
  With never a worry or care.

In Three Mighty Leaps

A FICTION STORY by Hilda V. Richardson

"GOT 'IM!" Paul Wilson called to Brian Vail, as he scooped up a frog in his net and dumped it in a basket. He waded over to Brian and handed his friend the net.

After Brian had caught his frog, he stood peering into the basket. "Let's trade frogs," he said at last.

"What for?" Paul asked.

"Yours is larger and prettier," replied Brian.

"Larger and prettier!" Paul snorted. "What's that got to do with how far a frog will jump?"

"Nothing," admitted Brian. "I guess I just like him best."

"Well," mused Paul, rubbing his chin, "since you're my best friend, I'll trade."

"Thanks," Brian said, grinning. "I'm going to name mine Croak!"

"I'll call mine Warts," decided Paul.

The boys carried the frogs home and put them in a specially made shallow pond covered with wire netting.

"Remember, we've got to make them practice jumping every day. The contest is just two weeks away," Paul said.

"What do we feed them?" Brian asked.

"Bumblebees are best," Paul replied.

"Bumblebees!" Brian exclaimed. "How can we catch enough bees?"

"We can always feed them earthworms," Paul said with an air of authority. "But they probably aren't hungry yet."

"How come you know so much about frogs?" Brian asked.

"Grandpa entered frogs in the annual frog jumping contest at Angels Camp for 25 years. Lots of times he won first prize. He taught me all I know about frogs."

"Where's Angels Camp?" Brian asked.

"It's in California. Grandpa said there's been an Annual Jumping Frog Jubilee there for over 40 years," Paul went on. "Frogs from around the world are entered, and hundreds of people go to watch."

"Sounds exciting," Brian admitted. "I hope someone in our school has a jumper good enough to send to Angels Camp."

After school the young trainers put Croak and Warts through their paces. Neither frog showed any eagerness to jump. The boys blew on them, pushed them, tickled them, and pounded the ground nearby to get their pets to jump.

Suddenly Warts jumped two feet and the boys fell back with whoops of laughter.

"How did you make him jump?" Brian cried.

"It must have been the stomping," Paul said.

"I'll try it," Brian said. Croak jumped too, but not in a straight line. "Leaping lizards—I mean frogs! Maybe our frogs aren't jumpers!"

"Don't give up," Paul said. "There's only one week left. We'll have to begin starving them like Grandpa said he used to do."

The day of the school contest drew near, but Warts and Croak were as quiet as ever. They didn't show the slightest interest in making it to Angels Camp, or in winning any of the prize money for Jefferson school.

It was the hottest day of the season when the pupils and teachers of Jefferson school gathered to watch the frogs out-jump each other.

Children joked and giggled with excitement as the fifth-grade teacher read the rules: "All contestants must be amphibians of the frog variety. They must stay under water in the pond for 15 minutes before jumping. All jumpers must spring off the starting spot with all legs down."

The first entry turned out to be a huge toad and was disqualified.

A number of others refused to move. After much coaxing and pleading, Brian's Croak jumped five feet —in a crooked line. The crowd whistled and shouted, and Brian swelled with pride. So far, his was best.

Paul's turn came last. He took Warts from the pond and slipped him some bumblebee morsels, then set him down on the spot. Warts squatted, panting in the sunshine. Paul stroked his back and whispered. "Come on, Warts! Show them how to jump!" Then he stood up and stomped his foot with all his might close behind the frog.

Instantly there was a flash of flying webbed feet! In three mighty leaps Warts covered nine feet!

The crowd went wild. Paul's classmates rushed to congratulate him. Paul dived among the onrushing feet to rescue Warts before he got trampled.

"You did it!" Brian yelled, jumping up and down. "You won!"

"Congratulations, Paul," said Miss Taylor. "Warts will jump for our school at Angels Camp!"

"Yea!" shouted the crowd. "Three cheers for Warts and Paul!"

All Paul could do was grin and stroke Warts' back. He felt happy deep inside because his frog was going to Angels Camp.

On the way home, Paul watched his friend's excitement gradually fade. "What's wrong?" he asked.

"Warts is really my frog," Brian finally blurted out.

"Your frog!" Paul exclaimed.

"I caught him," Brian insisted.

"But it was your idea to trade. You liked my frog best because he was bigger and prettier."

Brian didn't speak the rest of the way home. He turned into his driveway without saying good-bye.

"Warts won," Paul announced as he walked into his house.

His mother stopped peeling potatoes and stared at Paul. "Warts won? Then why the gloom?"

"In the beginning, Brian caught Warts. Then he wanted to trade because he liked my frog best. Now that Warts won, he wants to claim him."

"Mmmm," Paul's mother said. "That's very unfair of Brian."

"If I do nothing, I'll lose my best friend," Paul

fretted. "If I tell them at school it was his frog, it will make me look dishonest. I don't know what to do."

"Your grandfather always said that when he had a problem too big to solve himself, he turned it over to the Lord," his mother said.

"Grandpa was smart, wasn't he, Mom? Thanks for reminding me."

Paul was late getting to sleep that night. "I'm leaving it up to You, God. You're a lot wiser than I am. Please, please show me what to do."

Next morning he went off to school, whistling. He had an idea. He stopped at Brian's house as usual. Brian was just leaving, so Paul fell in step with his silent friend.

Halfway to school he cleared his throat and spoke. "I have an idea."

"Yeah?" Brian brightened.

"Today I'm going to tell Miss Taylor that we want Warts listed as belonging to both of us. It will appear that way in the newspaper write-up and on the program at Angels Camp."

"Hey, that's great. I can see it now," Brian said. " 'Warts, owned by Paul Wilson and Brian Vail, is the winner of Jefferson School Frog Jumping Contest. He will be entered at Angels Camp Jubilee!' "

Paul grinned at his friend's enthusiasm. So what if he had to share Warts' honor. At least Brian would know that a Christian will go more than halfway.

Brian turned and looked at his friend a moment, then said quietly, "Thanks."

The boys shook hands and ran the rest of the way to school to find Miss Taylor.

Laura Helps the Squirrel Family

A TRUE STORY by Gloria Truitt

EARLY in October Laura Truitt climbed out of bed and raised her window shade. The sun was struggling to peek through thick clouds. It looked cold and wintry out. Laura shivered.

It seemed like just yesterday that she was picking gold and red leaves off the large trees in their yard to decorate her room. Now the leaves that danced across the ground with each gust of wind were brown and dry.

Laura put on her jeans and chose her warmest sweater. "What a gloomy Saturday," she thought. "It's too cold for a bike ride. And what else is there to do this time of year?"

Mother and Daddy were already eating breakfast when she entered the kitchen. She plopped onto a chair and after praying reached for a piece of toast, mumbling, "This will probably be the most boring day of my life."

"Oh, I wouldn't say that," Daddy commented. "By the looks of things, I'd say we're going to get our first snow today!"

Mother quickly agreed. "I've never seen a more wintery looking sky in October," she added.

"Well, I hope it does snow!" Laura exclaimed, "and keeps right on snowing. Then, at least, there'll be something to do. Autumn is so in-between."

After helping Mother with the dishes, Laura decided to walk to the park. As she went out, she grabbed her tennis racket. "Maybe I can find someone who'd like to play," she said, doubtfully.

But the park was deserted and Laura felt shivery. She hurried home, and stood inside rubbing her hands together, saying, "Brrrr! It's cold out there! You were right, Mother and Daddy. It's snowing!"

Laura and Mother watched from the window as a carpet of white began to cover the backyard. Soon the slats of the redwood fence looked as if they were wearing rounded caps, and the once bare tree branches were frosted with puffs of white.

By late afternoon, it had stopped snowing. Laura hurried to find her jacket and boots. This time she grabbed a pair of mittens from the back porch cabinet where they had been stored during the summer.

The snow glittered like diamonds under the fading afternoon sun which had finally broken out of its cloud cover. Although the air was cold, it smelled fresh and clean. Laura ran through the snow. Then she looked up at Mother who was watching from a window.

"Watch this!" Laura yelled as she fell backwards onto the soft snow. Then she fanned her arms and legs back and forth to make angel patterns.

Brushing herself off, she scooped up a handful of snow and formed it into a ball. She tossed it at one of the trees and hit the trunk on target. As the snow went *splat,* Laura saw a movement on a high branch.

She stepped closer to see what it was. There, on a limb, sat the squirrel family who lived in the tree. They often came down to chat with Laura. Though Laura couldn't understand squirrel language, she would pretend to chatter back.

Laura loved to watch the squirrels scurry up and down the tree trunk. When they leaped from branch to branch, she and the rest of the Truitts would laugh with delight—even Laura's baby brother. But today the squirrel family seemed afraid. They sat quietly with their bushy tails strangely still.

Laura sensed that something was wrong. She ran into the house calling, "Mother, something's wrong with the squirrels! They're acting so strangely! Do you think they could be sick?"

Mother thought for a moment before she answered. "No, I don't think they're sick," she said at last. "It could be that they're disturbed about the snow. It has covered all the acorns on the ground. It may be that they had not had enough time to gather their full supply for winter food, and they don't know what to do."

As Mother spoke, tears gathered in Laura's eyes. "We've got to help them, Mother!" she cried. "We can't let them go hungry this winter. Jesus says we should help everyone. Don't you think He means little animals too?"

Mother nodded. "I'm sure He does. And we *should* help them."

Laura hugged Mother, than ran to the garage for a shovel while Mother hurried to get her coat. They scooped away the deep snow first with the shovel. Then, with their hands, they uncovered hundreds of acorns. These they placed in a crook of the big tree.

From a limb above, the squirrels watched with interest. Now and then they chattered excitedly. When Laura and Mother could find no more acorns, they went back into the house. They watched the busy squirrels from the window. Until dark, the squirrels scampered up and down the tree, carrying the acorns to their home in a hollow, high up.

"I'm so glad we helped them," Laura said, sighing with contentment. "Now they'll have enough food to last all winter."

Mother hugged Laura. "I'm glad too," she said, laughing.

Just then Laura glanced out of the window. "Look!" she exclaimed. "I think they're trying to tell us something."

Sure enough, the squirrel family sat on a branch, happily waving their bushy tails, as if to say *thank-you*.

Trouble for Biddy

A TRUE STORY by Norman E. King

SARAH was the daughter of early pioneers in the United States. They were homesteaders and lived out on the Midwestern prairies.

Often Sarah was lonely. The closest farm was several miles away. No children lived there so Sarah had to play alone. She had no toys except an old rag doll.

One day Sarah made a friend—a chicken. Her parents had brought a few chickens with them to their new home. The first spring the hens hatched several chicks. One little bird almost died. Sarah found it one morning. The other chicks had pecked it almost to death. It could hardly stand up and didn't have the strength to eat.

Sarah felt sorry for the chick. She took it into the house and put it in a box. She smoothed salve on its sores. Then she fed it and gave it water.

She named the chicken Biddy.

At first Biddy seemed to grow weaker and weaker. But Sarah didn't give up. Every day she put food into the chick's mouth. Using a clean quill—like a straw —she gave it water. She continued to care for Biddy's sores.

Biddy didn't die. After a while she got so she could stand up. Soon she began to eat by herself. But she liked best to eat out of Sarah's hand. Biddy seemed to know Sarah was her friend.

After a month or so, Biddy was able to go out into the yard. By now Sarah's parents had many fine chickens, but none was healthier than Biddy.

And Biddy was Sarah's good friend. As soon as Sarah came outside, Biddy would follow her. Even if Sarah took long walks, Biddy came along, riding on Sarah's shoulder.

But as Biddy grew older, she spent less time with Sarah. One day Sarah realized she hadn't seen Biddy for a couple of days. Sarah was worried. She hunted for Biddy and found her pet sitting on a nest out in the tall grass beyond the sod barn. In the nest were six smooth eggs.

Finally the great day came. Six chicks hatched! Sarah was the proudest, happiest girl in the Midwest. Biddy clucked happily, showing off the chicks.

When the chicks were old enough, Biddy brought them to the farmyard. Back and forth the young hen walked, clucking proudly so that everyone would notice them. Soon the new chicks became Sarah's friends too. Sarah was a very happy girl. She wasn't

lonesome anymore. Whenever she had any spare moments, she went out to play with her feathered friends.

Then one afternoon the western sky began to redden. A west wind brought the strong smell of smoke. Sarah knew right away what was wrong. Prairie fire!

Her father hurried and got out the team of horses and the plow. Quickly, he plowed a strip around the farm buildings. He explained that the grass nearby wasn't as high as the grass farther away. The fire would not be as strong when it came near them. Plowing a strip of sod would easily keep it from their buildings, and the fire would pass them without harming them.

In the excitement, Sarah forgot about Biddy and her chicks. The fire came closer and closer. Sarah soon felt its scorching heat. Would the plowed strip hold back the flames?

Just as her father had explained, the fire died down when it came up to the plowed strip. It went around the farmyard, then caught speed. Tall flames leaped as the wind whipped them eastward.

Sarah and her parents dropped to their knees and thanked God for His protection. Then they walked around the yard to see what the fire had done. All around was black and charred and smoking.

Suddenly Sarah thought of Biddy. Where was she? Where were the chicks? She ran to the sod barn. The cattle were there. The other chickens were safe too. But Biddy and her chicks were missing.

Sarah began to cry as she ran out to look around. Biddy was nowhere in sight. Sarah remembered the place where Biddy had made her nest. It was out beyond the barn, beyond the plowed strip.

Sarah ran to the nest. "Biddy!" she cried, stooping over the blackened body of her pet hen. "Oh, Biddy, you must not have known how to escape." Sarah sobbed as she picked up the dead hen. To her amazement, under Biddy's body nestled the six chicks. All were safe and unhurt. Biddy had died so her chicks might live.

In the same way, Jesus gave His life that we might find safety in Him. He died and took our punishment for our sins. If we trust in Him, God will forgive our sins and spare our lives. The fire of eternal punishment is far, far worse than a prairie fire! Won't you trust Jesus today?

The Gift

by Gloria A. Truitt

Late into autumn I went for a stroll,
Taking along mother's old, wooden bowl.
I was looking for acorns to string on a string,
So I could make mother some beads and a ring.
Just six weeks to Christmas, the calendar said . . .
(And such a short time between homework and bed.)
Then under an oak tree I found a surprise,
Hundreds of acorns, just perfect in size!

In a flurry I'd filled mother's bowl to the brim,
When a sad, baby squirrel I spied on a limb.
Below him his family was scampering around,
Frantically searching for what *I* had found.
I wondered what caused such an unhappy mood,
Then quickly I realized I'd taken their food!
While watching them scurry in frightened alarm,
I said very softly, "I meant you no harm."

On Christmas I wrapped up a shoe box instead,
Enclosing a note to my mother that read . . .
"I wanted to make you some jewelry to wear,
But I left it for all of the squirrels to share.
Next springtime I'll visit my animal friends,
For they'll still be alive when the long winter ends.
What acorns they've left, I'll collect in the spring,
And *then* I shall make you some beads and a ring!"

Fourteen Days in an Attic

A TRUE STORY

JOHN BRENTZ was a Christian reformer in Germany in the days of Martin Luther. Many rulers in the land hated Martin Luther and hated John Brentz too. Among them was the emperor, Charles V.

The emperor wanted to stop Brentz from preaching to the people that Jesus, God's Son, was their only means of having their sins forgiven. Like so many, the emperor hoped to get to heaven through his good works and the money he gave to the church. He did not want to be told the truth—that God had provided the blood of Jesus as the only covering for sins.

In order to stop Brentz from preaching, Emperor Charles V sent a troop of Spanish cavalry out to find and arrest him. But friends of Brentz heard of the ᴡicked plot and warned him before the cavalry reached ᴛ city.

When Brentz heard that the soldiers were after him, he fell on his knees and asked God to tell him what he should do. He knew he was in great danger. As he prayed, God said to him, "Take a loaf of bread, go into the upper town, and where you find a door open, enter and hide under the roof."

The reformer hurried out to obey the Lord. He bought the loaf of bread and did find an open door in the upper part of the town. Without anyone seeing him, he climbed the stairs to the attic of the building. A big pile of lumber and straw was stored there. He squeezed into a little corner behind it all.

The very next day, the soldiers entered the town. They guarded all gates leading into it and began a thorough search of every room in every house throughout the entire city.

They stuck their swords and spears into bedding and any piles of straw they found, to make sure John Brentz wasn't hiding there. The search went on for 14 days, until every house in the city had been searched.

The house in which the reformer was hiding was the very last one the soldiers examined. When they came to the little room at the top of the building where Brentz was hiding, they thrust their spears into the straw. But because the straw did not go to the very back of the room, their spears did not touch Brentz. He held his breath while they were there, but finally, with joy, heard the leader of the soldiers say, "March! He is not here."

But how had John Brentz managed to stay alive for

14 days with only a loaf of bread? Well, to his amazement, the very first day of his hiding, a hen came up to the attic and laid an egg in the straw.

The next day the hen did the same thing, and the next, and the next. For 14 days that hen came and laid an egg a day. The fifteenth day the hen did not come back. That was the day Brentz could go free because he heard the people in the street saying, "They are gone at last!"

So, through a hen, God supplied food for one of His children during days of danger.

Watch Out for Butter

A FICTION STORY by Craig Massey

DAVE HILLIARD was working on his bike in the driveway when Mr. Ballfant, the nextdoor neighbor, came storming over. "David Hilliard! Your rabbit is in my garden again!" Mr. Ballfant roared.

David leaped up and dashed out to Mr. Ballfant's garden. Sure enough, there was Fluffy, enjoying Mr. Ballfant's beet tops. David grabbed up Fluffy, and carried her to the hutch, wondering grimly how to keep the rabbit in her cage.

It wouldn't be so bad, he told himself, as he trudged back to Mr. Ballfant's to apologize, *but it seems as if something happens almost every day to make Mr. Ballfant angry. And he sure does get angry!*

Three times that week, Fluffy had managed to squeeze out of her cage. And Monday, Dave's football had sailed right through Mr. Ballfant's garage window when Dave was playing in the yard with friends. Yesterday, Dave fell off his bike into the Ballfant's prize roses. Each time Mr. Ballfant had stormed over as mad as a hornet.

He wasn't much pleasanter this time when David offered his apology. "You make me boil!" Mr. Ballfant yelled. "You're supposed to be Christians yet you're thoughtless and irresponsible! I couldn't have worse neighbors!"

David didn't say a word. What could he say? He felt terrible. His family had prayed that the Ballfants would realize that they needed Christ Jesus in their lives. But everything seemed to be going wrong.

David's Dad had replaced the broken window himself, and David had promised to work off the cost of the flowers and vegetables by mowing the Ballfant's lawn. But nothing seemed to satisfy the angry man.

"I'd better get to work on Fluffy's cage and make sure she doesn't get out again," he decided.

David had just stepped into the garage when his mother called him. "Dave, Todd is on the phone," she said.

A moment later Dave was saying, "Hi, Todd."

"Hey, Dave," Todd began, "how about doing me a favor."

Dave hedged, "Well, I might. What is it?"

"I have to go away this afternoon and need someone to take care of Butter, my pet goat. I can't leave him home because he always chews the rope in two and gets into trouble. No one will be home."

Dave grinned. He liked the goat. He and Todd had

nearly split their sides laughing over the animal's antics. Yes, Butter could cheer the gloomiest guy. "Sure, bring him over," he told Todd.

Just as he hung up the phone, his mother called to him, "Dave, I have to go shopping and want you to watch Kathy for me."

Always good-natured, Dave readily agreed to watch his three-year old sister. "Sure, Todd is bringing Butter over," he said. "I'll take care of them together."

"David Hilliard," his mother said, coming into the hall, "don't you let that goat get near Kathy! You know he butts people."

"I'll be careful!" David promised.

At about two in the afternoon Todd left Butter with Dave. The goat was pretty—a soft tan with slender legs. Dave leaned over and patted the animal. "You may be pretty, but those eyes of yours are sure full of mischief," David said to Butter. "Just don't try anything because I'll be watching!"

Butter tossed his head playfully, and let out a long, "Ba-a-a-a-a!"

Just then Mother came out on her way to go shopping. She brought Kathy out with her. "David, don't you let that goat near this baby, now. Remember!" she warned before she got into the car.

"I won't. I'll tie him by the garage and keep Kathy on the front porch," Dave called as his mother backed out of the driveway.

But Butter didn't want to be tied. He tossed his head in anger when Dave tried to pull him. It took a lot of work to tie the rope securely. And by the time he was done and had returned to the front porch, Kathy was gone.

"Kathy," he called, racing around the house. "Kathy, where are you?" He finally found her in the kitchen with the peanut butter jar. Her face and hair and clothes were smeared with it.

"Oh, Kathy, look at you," he groaned. "This is going to be a busy afternoon, I can see," he said as he washed off the peanut butter.

When she was clean, he took her to the front porch again and set her on the swing with a picture book. At that moment, he heard a loud "Ba-a-a-a" and looked up. To his dismay, Butter was loose again and in their petunias.

"Get out of the flowers!" he yelled, waving his arms.

Butter looked up in surprise and trotted off down the street with Dave after him. "Stop!" Dave called. "Butter, come back here!"

After a 10-minute chase, Dave finally caught the rope, dangling around the goat's neck. On the way home, he suddenly remembered Kathy. "Wow, I hope she's all right," he said as he tugged at the rope.

She was. She was watching Mr. Ballfant mix a bucket of tar to patch his roof.

Once again Dave tied Butter and for about half an hour he had some peace as Kathy played contentedly with her doll and Butter slept.

When the phone rang, Dave dashed into the house and answered it. It turned out to be a wrong number. He walked back out on the porch to find Kathy laughing. "Goat all gone!" she said.

"Oh, no!" Dave gasped. "Not again! Where did he go?"

"There," Kathy pointed to the back of the house.

Dave ran around the house and almost bumped into the goat.

With a startled, "Ba-a-a-a!" Butter began to run, but Dave leaped for the rope and managed to catch him right away this time.

Out of breath from the tussle, Dave sat on the ground for a couple of minutes. "Wow, if I were Todd, I'd buy you a chain so you couldn't chew yourself free all the time," he told the goat.

"Guess I better see how Kathy is doing," he said, getting up. But Kathy wasn't on the porch. "Where are you?" Dave called again.

"Here," her baby voice came from behind him.

Dave swung around in time to see her lean over Mr. Ballfant's bucket of tar. "No, Kathy! Don't touch," he called. But too late. Delighted with the black tar, Kathy dipped both hands in, then pulled them out, dripping the thick liquid all down herself.

Dave grabbed her up just in time to keep her from doing it again. "Honey, you mustn't play in Mr. Ballfant's tar. You'll make him angry," he scolded. "Here we've been praying that he would accept Jesus as his Saviour. He already thinks we Christians are troublemakers. I'm sure glad he isn't around."

A loud "Ba-a-a-a" from behind made David whirl around just in time to see Butter trotting toward him with his head lowered.

Dave set Kathy down quickly as he shouted, "Stop!"

at the goat. But it was no use. The goat playfully tossed his head and butted Dave. The blow wasn't hard enough to hurt, but it sent Dave flying backwards "kerplunk" into the bucket of tar.

The sticky stuff splattered in all directions. Kathy giggled. And before Dave could stop her she sat down in a pool of tar. Butter seemed to be enjoying the fun and started to toss his head again.

Dave pulled himself up out of the bucket, and dripping tar, managed to get hold of Butter's rope again. "Oh, what will Mother say when she sees us," David wailed. "And what will Mr. Ballfant do when he sees this terrible mess!"

Just then Dave heard someone laughing. He looked toward the street but no one was there. He looked back of the house but no one was there. He searched everywhere, but not a soul was in sight. And yet the laughter kept on and on.

Suddenly he looked up. To his amazement, he saw Mr. Ballfant sitting on his roof. He was holding his sides and laughing as if he'd burst.

It was the first time Dave had ever seen Mr. Ballfant laugh. Astonished, Dave sat down right there on the grass, holding the goat. Mr. Ballfant came down a ladder nearby. "That was the funniest thing I ever saw," he said, wiping tears of laughter from his eyes.

"I'm sure sorry for all the mess," Dave said, soberly.

"It was worth the fun," Mr. Ballfant said. "I saw the whole thing." And he began laughing again.

"Then you heard what I said to Kathy too?" Dave asked, feeling his face grow hot.

"Yes, and I must say that if your God can keep you from getting angry with all the trouble you've had this afternoon, I guess I'd better find out more about Him. I sure need someone to help me keep my temper."

"I'll be glad to tell you about Jesus," Dave said, hanging on to the struggling goat. "Just let me tie up Butter again. And, Kathy, you stay right here."

"Don't worry, I'll hang onto her," Mr. Ballfant said, picking up the little girl, tar and all. "I think you can use a little help too."

The Ostrich

by Gloria A. Truitt

An ostrich is a giant bird . . .
   You couldn't say he's small!
Sometimes he weighs 300 pounds
   And measures eight feet tall!
Though he has feathers and two wings,
   An ostrich cannot fly
Like other birds who dip and glide,
   Exploring God's blue sky.
Despite the fact we'd never call
   This bird a flying ace,
He runs at 40 miles an hour . . .
   Now, that's a speedy pace!

Inky

told by Phil Erickson
written by Delnora M. Erickson

I'M NOT sure who gave Inky to us. It was at a time when I thought I had to have a dog. However, there was a leash law in Spokane, Washington where we lived then, and Mother said I couldn't have a dog until we could fence in the yard.

Inky was a Manx cat. He was a tiny kitten when he came, but it didn't seem any time until he was a huge cat. He was all black except for a white face and chest and two white paws. Unlike most Manx cats he had a long tail.

Everyone in the family loved Inky, but to me he was more than a pet. He was a friend and companion. We wrestled and played games together. Seemed like he could almost talk my language at times.

He knew his name and would come when I called him. If he was outside and wanted to come into the house, he would stand on his hind legs and rattle the doorknob until someone let him in. He loved to sit on the lamp table and look out the window. Everyone agreed that he was very smart. And he was a fighter! He would take on any dog in the neighborhood. Dogs learned early to respect him.

But one night tragedy came to Inky. In the middle of the night, he jumped up on my bed and woke me up. I opened my eyes to see this blood-covered cat sitting on my chest, asking for help. Immediately, I got up and ran to wake up my mother. Together we tried to make him comfortable in his box until morning. I slept very little the rest of the night. My heart ached for the cat. I knew he must be hurting terribly.

I don't know whether he was in a fight or a car hit him. His jaw was mangled and he had many bruises. We found a trail of blood leading through the pup tents my brother and I had outdoors. It led to each basement window and finally to the door of the coal bin where he had managed to get in. Then he came to our basement bedroom.

That morning, the family talked over Inky's condition. Everyone but me thought he should be taken to the veterinarian and put to sleep.

"But maybe the vet could fix him up," I pleaded. "Can't we at least try him?"

"It would cost too much," Father said. "Inky would have to stay at the vet's for weeks and then he might not be all right. That cat has been hurt badly."

I couldn't bear the thought of Inky dying. He had become such an important part of my life. "If I pay his way, can we at least ask the vet to try?" I asked. I had no idea how much it might cost, but the money didn't seem important right then.

"That would be expecting a lot, wouldn't it?" asked Mother. "Where would you get the money?"

"The Hansons are going on vacation this week. Mr. Hanson asked me to take care of their lawn while they're gone. I can get other jobs mowing lawns. Please let me do it."

"OK," Father said, "but remember Inky is your responsibility. I can't put that much money into a cat." Mother drove us to the veterinarian, and he examined Inky. "I don't know—he's badly hurt," the vet said. "But I'll try. I'll have to wire his jaw together, and he'll have to stay here until it heals."

I was so happy to have him willing to put Inky back together again that I thought the battle was already won. We drove home and I hurried out to find all the jobs I could.

It was July and the weather was hot, but I spent many many hours mowing lawns. I was doing it for Inky so it didn't seem hard. At the end of a week I went back to see how he was doing.

The vet shook his head when he saw me. "We were doing great," he said, "but last night he managed to loosen the wire in his jaw, so I had to fix it all over again. It's going to be at least two more weeks, and then we'll see how it heals."

I was disappointed but not discouraged. I went home and hunted up more lawns to cut. Mr. Hanson came home and paid me well for taking care of his.

At the end of the three weeks I finally had Inky home. And I had proudly paid the bill from my earnings.

Inky looked different. Mother said his face was so ugly now that she didn't like to look at him. His jaw was crooked and it did give him a strange look, but the family soon got used to it. Once more Inky was part of our household.

Six months later my Father was transferred to Clinton, Iowa. It was Christmas and my older sisters and brother were home from college and Bible school for the holidays. The next week we were to drive south through California and leave the girls at their schools, then go on to Iowa. Only my younger sister and I would be going to Iowa with my parents.

When the news of the transfer first came, Mother asked me how I felt about the move. Changes in the middle of the school year were always hard. We had had many of them through the years.

"It's all right," I said. "I don't mind moving if I can take Inky with me."

To drive that far in a crowded car with a cat, even one as well-behaved as Inky, was something unheard of in our family. But Mother said, "We'll try, but I can't promise we'll get to Iowa with him."

I was overjoyed. I didn't doubt that we would make it all the way with the cat. I bought a little harness and leash for him.

We packed the car and started out. Our first coffee break was in Oregon. We piled out of the car. When we returned a short time later, the leash and harness lay on the sidewalk—no Inky. My heart sank.

We fanned out in every direction, calling the cat. We all returned disappointed. There was no sign of Inky. Then I saw him. He was sitting on the front tire under the car's fender.

We all got into the car and started out again. That night we stayed in a motel on the border of California. We bedded Inky down in the small kitchen, but he made so much noise, no one could sleep.

Mother opened the door and put him outside. My faith wasn't very strong that night. I had a hard time going to sleep. I was afraid I would never see him again. Would someone take him in and feed him or would he wander around and starve to death?

The next morning when we opened the door, Inky was sitting on the hood of the car waiting for us.

"There's one thing sure," said Mother, "we aren't going to lose the cat."

We reached Iowa. The weather was very cold. Within a week Father was able to rent a house. Our furniture arrived and we moved in. But we didn't all live happily ever after with the smartest most lovable cat in the world. In a few months there was another problem.

We were to move to the place where Father was chaplain. Everything about that move was good—except for one thing. The manager said, "No pets." They had had a lot of trouble with animals on the post.

"I'm sorry, Phil," said Mother. "We need to move there. You'll have to make other plans for Inky."

I had made friends with an elderly neighbor lady

who lived across the street. When I told her my problem she said, "I'd love to have Inky. Why don't you bring him over the day you move?"

She was a kind person. I knew he would have a good home. One of the movers said, when he saw the cat, "I'd like to have him for my children." But I told him I had promised him to the lady across the street.

We were nicely settled in our new home when a call came from the neighbor lady. "You'll have to come and get Inky," she said. "I'd like to keep him but I broke my arm. I'm afraid I might trip over him."

Another family council. "I don't know the name of the man who said he would like to have the cat," said Mother "but I think the other mover called him Carl." She called the moving company and was soon in touch with the right man.

"I'll be happy to have that cat," he told her. "I'll go over and get him after work tonight."

I never saw Inky again. But I was grateful that God had given me a treasure of love in Inky. And He had taught me a lesson through Inky's accident that I'd never forget: I learned that even as the Lord could take care of a pet cat, He could take care of me.

In a way, Inky was like the sparrows Jesus mentioned when He said, "Are not five sparrows sold for two cents? And yet not one of them is forgotten before God . . . Do not fear; you are of more value than many sparrows" (Luke 12:6-7, NASB).